Walk Tall

Arrival at Rawnpore

Walk Tall

A tale of love and loyalty

Jean Hamilton

With love to James
from
Jean Hamilton.

1989
D. BROWN & SONS LIMITED
COWBRIDGE · WALES

Dedicated
to those I love

© 1989 Jean Hamilton

ISBN 0 905928 96 2

DESIGNED AND PRINTED IN WALES BY
D. Brown and Sons Ltd., Cowbridge and Bridgend, Glamorgan

Introduction

This small volume is a picture of "working-class" life at the turn of the 20th century, and seeks to show how poor people, ordinary people (even as many do now) could enjoy a life full of interest, adventure, love and laughter, despite experiencing great suffering, physical and mental, which at that time could not be alleviated by the wonder drugs, brilliant surgery, and amazing technology of today. There was no Welfare State and, I advocate, no regression to such poverty and suffering. Nevertheless, there was great achievement in every field of life—with courage and neighbourly love much in evidence. Today, one's senses are assailed by the grandiose extravaganzas of much of modern life, encased in noise and materialism, divorce, the outrageous and the false anodyne of alcohol and drugs. So many are seeking but never finding Peace and Happiness.

Is mankind any the better or any safer, and happier for having landed men on the moon, for having created "spies" in the sky or for having bounced straight into our living-rooms pictures from the ends of the earth?

Is the human soul any better or any different between then and now? We still need human courage and real grit to overcome the enormity of our present-day problems.

I turned to the oldest people I remember to find a possible key to this question and now I make a plea for the enduring quality of life to return.

Glossary

Anna = former Indian coin, small in value
Ayah = child's nurse
Angrezi-log = English people
Budmarsh = rascal
Burra Bungalow = men's quarters
Chatti = large earthenware water-pot
Dhobi = laundryman
Dâk = bungalow inn, where post could be collected
Ekka = light two-wheeled trap
Ghari = a horse-drawn vehicle
Koss = about two miles
Punkah = piece of matting, pulled by a rope to make a breeze
Topee = pith helmet-shaped sun-hat
Tiffin = lunch

Acknowledgements

To Mr R. D. Whitaker of D. Brown & Sons Ltd., for his help and advice
and to my dear friend Ruth for the sketches.

PART I

I

He was a poor little soul, limping down the hill, stumbling in the heather roots, as he took the long, hard way home. He ached all over, every nerve and muscle hurt and, worst of all, his pride was hurt. It was so unjust.

At length, he came to the little burn which tumbled down the side of the ben. Despite his pain, he was aware that the day was bright and sunny, and that the lark was singing his heart out, right above his head, as though to comfort him. He looked around, nobody was in sight, so he took off his pants and, picking his steps very carefully, he waded out to the pool, under the great boulder. There was always some depth of water there. Thankfully, he sat down with care in the cool water. This pool was always a friend to him, in pleasure or in pain. Now, after the smarting lessened, it proved his salvation.

Now, he could think. At nine-and-three-quarter years it is easier to think when a smarting bottom is immersed in cool, peaty water, the lark is singing and the peewit is trying to call his mate.

Davie was a quiet child who could put up with a lot, without fuss or complaint, but too much is too much. He was used to slaps and hunger and abuse, but today was different. Shame overwhelmed him, injustice burnt into his very soul. It was not so much the lick of the strap, even if its five fingers had been soaked in water, then allowed to dry and harden, it was the awful shock.

A most affectionate, friendly child, with large, trusting blue eyes, he felt a slow, dull hate for two people take possession of his whole heart and mind; hate for the dominie and hate for Archie McCulloch. It was typical of the boy that he did not include soul—for part of him was aware that hate should not possess his very soul.

His first instinct had been to run away to the moor, mile after mile, then just lie down and die. At the thought of dying, his mother's face appeared before him. His poor mother had done her best last night, after the young ones were in bed. He, the eldest of six—and another well on the way, had sat with his mother drinking a mug of strong, sweet tea.

9

'Mum, I don't want to go to school tomorrow. I'll dig the back garden for you, instead. Willie and the others will all be there and I won't be missed.'

'Indeed you will, Davie, you must go—why not?'

After a good deal of persuasion and a piece of bread and dripping, his mother had wormed out the reason. 'She was clever, she was, a fellow never realised he was telling what he didn't want to tell—until it was too late.'

'You see, the Inspector is coming tomorrow morning and the domi-nie told us, that we must go dressed in our best. He said that there would be a thrashing for anyone who did not. Willie, Meggie and Neil have clothes from the cousins, but there was nothing in the parcel from Inveraray to fit me. So I'll just stay at home.'

The mother's eyes clouded with sorrow. Of all her children, Davie was the one nearest to her heart, her first born—born of true love. The others were also her children and Neil's, of course, but they had arrived so fast, year by year—they just seemed different—Davie was special. With six children already and little money coming in, she had to keep food in their stomachs, clothes were a luxury. Now and then a big parcel of garments would arrive from her sister, but they were mostly girls' garments. Boys always seemed to wear their trousers out and they could not be passed on.

Neil was blacksmith to the laird, Sir Geoffrey Milne, but the laird forgot that it was hard to feed and clothe eight, on twenty-five-and-sixpence per week. Fortunately, they had the small, terraced cottage free. Now, she could no longer take in washing, she was too far "gone" again.

Poor wee Davie, sparing her all he could—and him not yet ten years old. She should have left him and Meggie in Inveraray with Susan, her sister, who had no children. Neil, of course, would not hear of it, but they would have been better off.

'What's wrong with your corduroy shorts? I washed them yester-day.'

'They have a big hole in the back, Mum. I couldn't wear them for the Inspector's visit.'

'Well, go to bed now, Davie. I'll see what can be done.'

So his beloved mother had sat up for hours, patching and pressing his shorts.

'My, could she patch, his mother—you could hardly tell—just that the patch was slightly darker at the seat.'

Now, Davie suddenly noticed that the lark had stopped singing and that the heat was going out of the sun. His mother would be worrying about him. Meggie and the others would have told her about the thrashing, before the whole school, even in front of the little ones. So he put on his shorts, socks and boots, and, much helped by the cool water, he ran down the hill towards the village. He would have to face them soon, so when he came in sight of the cottages, he slowed down. He felt he had lost something that day. Years later, he realised it was his natural dignity. So now, he trailed home like a blackbird with a hanging wing—in and out the bushes, just putting off time. At last, he came to the spot where the burn ran into the river and he was at the mill and home. Away to the right was the manager's house and up the hill amid the trees stood the laird's mansion. However, it was the third cottage from the right which drew his attention.

'Aye, she was there,' he thought.

One hand was shading her eyes, the other supported the burden in her body. Davie called and gave his mother a wave; he was, after all, her eldest. He must put a good face on it. When he got nearer, she leant against the doorpost and just said, 'Come away in, laddie, I've kept your tea for you.'

This was her expression of intense sympathy—no meals were kept if you were late—only Neil's.

Tea-time was always at five, before father came home. He was a hard man, but just, always weary after heavy labour, starting at six each morning, summer and winter alike. He worked at least twelve hours daily—more if the master sent horses in late. The laird owned the paper mill, and horses sent to the smithy had always to be shod before morning.

The mother's arm was round Davie now and he was drawn into the unusual silence of the kitchen. They were all there except father—all home early from school that day. Even John at eleven months was quiet in his cot. All sensed the hurt.

'Have your tea now, Davie, you can tell me later!'

She did not offer him a stool, she realised he would have to stand to keep what dignity was left. So Davie drank the hot tea, well-sugared tonight, and ate the cold pork and potatoes, with more relish than he had thought possible.

'Was it your fault, Davie?'

'No, Mum,' piped up Meggie, 'it was the patch.'

'THE PATCH?'

It was later than they thought. There was a sudden scraping of boots at the door.

'There's father, let him eat first.'

But bush telegraph had been at work.

'And what's this story I hear about you, Davie? Is it true?'

'Yes, father.'

'What did you do, to deserve such a thrashing?'

Dear lovable Meggie could bear it no longer.

'It wasn't Davie's fault, father, it was Archie McCulloch's.'

At the sound of the name, Davie felt faint and sat down cautiously on the chair by the fire. As the droning of the voices went on, he relived the whole incident once more.

Archie was a great bully. He was swanking in his new grey suit and looked pointedly at the patch on Davie's trousers.

'The dominie warned us to be dressed for the Inspection,' he sneered.

The bell rang, the lines formed, Archie stuck out his foot and tripped up Davie. The master shouted, 'Come here, Cameron! Can't you stand in a line like the others?'

Then his cold gimlet eyes surveyed the blue-eyed, fair-haired lad and his voice trembled with anger. As he fell, Davie had felt a sharp tug at his shorts.

'Well, Cameron, have you no ears to hear? Repeat my last words to you all, yesterday!'

The whisper could hardly be heard.

'We were to come dressed, sir.'

'Line number one, march!'

In five minutes all were packed into the school hall, from the youngest to those in standard six.

Meggie's voice came back as through a haze.

'The auld deevil.'

'Mind your language, Meg!'

'He was a deevil, father,' said Willie.

'Yes?'

The voices faded out again, but with eyes closed, Davie still heard and saw the master.

When all the school was assembled in silence, one could hear a pin drop, for the dominie had made Davie take off his shorts before the whole school, girls as well as boys, and he had held up the breeks by the torn patch.

'NO-ONE but NO-ONE in this school will come on the day of inspection with a patch hanging off his pants.'

Then the merciless thrashing began.

'Father, we were all crying,' said Meggie. 'Jimmy Clayton, the pupil-teacher, pulled at the dominie's arm and managed, after a while, to take the strap from the master, because Davie was lying on the floor with his eyes shut.'

Father was a stern disciplinarian, but he was just. Although he had newly finished a thirteen hour day at the smiddy, he turned on his heel without a word and strode up the road, with obvious intent.

The banging and the knocking brought the dominie to his door, his napkin tucked into his collar and still chewing.

'Come outside, Mr. McNab, and I'll give you a taste of your own medicine. How dare you thrash my son without mercy, as you did today? How dare you injure him and shame him before the whole school, when he had done nothing wrong?'

McNab was no longer so arrogant.

'He disobeyed my orders.'

'Even if that were true, 'tis no excuse for unfair and vicious thrashing. He is cut on face, arms, legs and bottom. I shall report you for assault to the police.'

'Rules are rules, Cameron.'

'Aye, and understanding is understanding—I should think an elementary qualification for a headmaster.'

McNab's hands were shaking. This short, thickset highlander frightened him.

'I'll not soil my hands giving you a bloody nose, but if you ever lay a hand on any of my bairns again, I'll have the law on you. As for Davie, he won't be back; for with all your education, you're just a brute. Don't ever cross my path, night or day.'

Wearily he walked the mile home again. It had taken all the self-control he could muster to keep his strong hands off McNab, but even in his fury he knew restraint. In this unfair world, he would have been the guilty party, accused of assault, and he couldn't risk arrest.

'What happened, Neil?' asked Alice.

'Davie will not go back to school, I forbid it.'

But he is not yet ten, Neil, it's the law.'

'Woman! He WILL NOT go back! That is final. He will hammer for me.'

Well, there was no more to be said. Neil ate his cold meal without a grumble. The children were in bed. His mother had bathed and put vaseline on the ugly weals on Davie's legs and bottom, which were worse than his face and arms. He must have rolled himself into a ball to protect his head.

After having eaten, Neil went to look at Davie. Even he, was aghast at the terrible weals and wished silently, that he had given McNab a punching.

'Davie, you will stay in bed tomorrow, then we'll see. You won't go back to school.'

Davie was flushed and feverish for several days and was black and blue for weeks.

I'm sorry now, I didn't pound the blackguard, when I had the chance', admitted Neil to Alice.

And what of McNab's inspection?

The Inspector, stout, red-faced and breathing heavily, had descended at mid-afternoon from his gig. He tethered the animal to the rail of the playground and walked pompously to the school entrance, where McNab received him as Uriah Heep might have done. The same McNab would have made a good advertisement for hand-lotion.

The self important, so-called Inspector cast a cursory glance over the register, looked around and asked, 'Miss Fraser, where is she?'

'Unfortunately, sir, she is suffering from a heavy cold and had to return home.'

'Hmm. See that we engage less sickly female staff in future.'

Mentally, he thought that Clayton, the pupil-teacher, looked sullen and very white about the gills.

The children were very quiet, very obedient.

'I see some pinafores badly creased, and it is only three o'clock in the afternoon.'

McNab cringed.

The lordly Inspector made the school sing the first verse of the twenty-third Psalm.

'Probably the only one he knows himself,' thought young Clayton.

Then, to the relief of everyone, the visitor departed.

'Will you take tea at the schoolhouse, sir?'

'No, no, I'm dining with the Provost of Blairton tonight. Good afternoon.'

So much for the inspection, with all its farcical pretence of importance and so much for the outrageous scene of the morning, when a child was thrashed until he was only half-conscious. Young Clayton had had enough of egoists and sadists—bastards both of them. He departed at the earliest opportunity to work in Blairton. As for Miss Fraser, she too had had enough of McNab, and she went to help her sister who had a needlework shop.

To think that in 1860 McNab's only qualifications to teach, had been an interview with a few inspector-types, when he had to do three things: sing a psalm (hymns did not count), say a prayer, then give a talk on a Bible story. Clayton felt he was well out of it.

Davie need not have felt the shame he did. The whole village loved him—with the exception of the impossible McCullochs. He could walk with his head up. It was poor Mrs. McCulloch who suffered when she entered the local shop. She was ostracised and was heard to mutter, 'It wasn't my fault. I have to live with him.'

This brought the second great change to Davie's life. The first had been when he had to leave Inveraray. Neil had been a blacksmith not far from Inveraray and had met and married Alice, the youngest daughter of a modest crofter. They lived in a cottar house just outside the little town. Davie was born there and remained there, for five years. Meggie, his sister, was two years younger, and they had a wonderful life, little money, but much happiness.

A farrier of means set up in opposition and, having friends in high places, attracted most of the work for the horses of the castle. Neil, therefore, had to look elsewhere, or become a farmworker.

A cousin, who worked in a paper mill in Ruary, forty miles away towards Edinburgh, said that a blacksmith was needed at the mill. Neil decided to move there, an unfortunate decision for Alice and the children.

Young as he was, Davie had absorbed much of the atmosphere of the countryside. He had run around in his little Cameron kilt, been teased by the Campbells of the district, had learnt to imitate the thrush and the blackbird, had paddled in Loch Fyne and had loved it. Meggie, at three, knew many of the wild flowers. Aunt Susan and Uncle Alistair lived only two miles away on a small farm. Life was idyllic. Anywhere else would have suffered by comparison. They were all loath to leave their home. Alice and Neil had returned once on holiday, when there were three children and Neil a babe in arms. Aunt Susan had offered to keep Davie and Meggie 'for the summer' but Neil said, 'No, it would be too difficult for me to travel back for them in the autumn.'

As to this second change in his life, Davie was very glad to leave school, but dreaded working with his father in the blacksmith's shop. Neil was broad and strong, and in his heavy leather apron, with his sleeves rolled up and a red hot horseshoe in his tongs, was quite an awe-inspiring figure to a small son.

Davie was slight of build—with thin delicate features, blond curls and large, honest blue eyes. He favoured his mother's family.

He had to stand on a stool to use the hammer and he had little strength in his arms but he was useful to Neil who, in his heart, pitied his son having to work so hard at less than ten years of age. He gave him small items to hammer—poker handles or flat plates for door scrapers but it was still hot and hard.

Davie also ran errands, held horses waiting to be shod, kept the fire glowing and was at Neil's beck and call from six o'clock in the morning until six o'clock in the evening. Then there was a long walk to and from the cottage. After eating, he just tumbled into bed.

Sometimes when his father had to go to Craigallion, the laird's house, to fetch a horse, it would only be necessary for Davie to keep the fire going, so he had time then, to sit outside the smiddy door on a box, and watch the birds or a red squirrel in the copse across the road. When all was quiet, when there were no men or horses about, and especially when there was no hammering, they would show themselves and Davie liked to imagine that this was just for him. He received no money from his father and he expected none.

'My, you're a great wee singer,' he would say to a thrush, then try to imitate it. In winter he actually taught a thrush to take crumbs from his hand.

Meggie would make a detour coming from school and they would have a long chat, if father was engaged in conversation with someone else. Davie and Meggie had always been close and this friendship was to last a lifetime. Meggie would sometimes deliver messages from the village shop to the cottages and might receive a few sweets. Despite her own hunger, even at eight years old, she would always keep a few for Davie.

'Are you glad, Davie, not to be at school?'

'Aye, but some day I'll batter that Archie, it was his fault.'

'We have two new teachers, Davie, the others left. In the shop, I heard Mrs. Reevie saying it was because of you. They had a row with old McNab about what he did to you.'

Davie felt a glow of gratitude that anyone should care enough for him to do such a thing.

'That old deevil never looks at Willie or at me. It's as though we weren't there.'

2

Jimmy Geddes was a machineman at the paper mill. He was a kindly man of about forty-five and lived in a little cottage, set in a neat vegetable garden, just beyond the smiddy. He and his wife Sarah were childless. They worked hard in the garden and were modestly comfortable on his wage of thirty-five shillings and sixpence per week. They had chickens and ducks and were probably the happiest couple in Ruary. Sarah had been nanny at the laird's house and had married Jimmy when he was a beaterman.

After coming off night-shift, he would often stop at the smiddy, in the early morning, to pass the time of day with Neil. Neil would be bustling about while Davie used the bellows to get the fire going. There was a sharing of village gossip and the latest jokes, but it soon became apparent that it was Davie he really came to see. He had always liked the look of Neil's 'eldest'. The direct look from the honest blue eyes and the tilt of the chin, as though he were always listening. Indeed, he was. If a bird was singing, Davie always stopped to listen. Jimmy was a real countryman and when, one morning, he heard Davie imitating the song thrush so perfectly that the two seemed to be having a private conversation, he took a few minutes now and then to tell him about the different types of birds in the area; about those which migrated and those which stayed, about the cuckoo, and he even confided his great secret—that there was a kingfisher's nest down by the river. Jimmy had to be a bit careful, for Neil did not like time being wasted. He had, of course, heard of that merciless flogging, but said nothing—just gazed at the boy, his eyes dark with compassion. What chance did a youngster have, working as his father's dogsbody?

Now that the seventh child had arrived, Alice was looking more worn out than ever. In a two room and kitchen, where on earth did they all sleep? It was a blessing Ruary was so small—just a little village in the country. At least the air was fresh and clean.

Once, when Neil was away at the stables, Jimmy said:

'You will soon be eleven, Davie; do you want to be a blacksmith like your father?'

'Not really, I want to earn some money to help with the little ones.'

'Well, if you like, I will speak to your father. We need a lad at the

17

mill, for the most humble of jobs—sorting rags. It is a low and filthy job, Davie, but you would be on the payroll at three shillings and sixpence per week. Although you would loathe the job, the important thing is, that you would be in the mill and eligible for promotion as it came along. If you worked well, you could get quick promotion to cleaner things.'

Neil and Alice were quite happy to let Davie go—three shillings and sixpence per week would make all the difference to the weekly budget when there were two adults and seven children to feed.

Meggie said, 'You won't like being shut in, Davie, you like the birds so much.'

'Och, I'll go to the woods on Sundays and whistle with the blackie and the mavis.'

So Davie started at the lowest level in the paper mill, two days after his eleventh birthday.

Another boy of twelve worked with him. The rags were delivered to a big shed set apart from the mill. All kinds and conditions of rags were delivered at the far entrance by locals, by rag and bone men and by tinkers, all of whom were paid in coppers according to the quality and quantity of the rags delivered.

About ten small trucks stood along one wall of the shed, on rails. The boys had to sort the rags into the different trucks—cottons, linens, wool, mixed fibres, pale colours, dark colours, whites, jute sacking, and so on, because each type required different preparation. Buttons had to be removed—and buckles. The boys were allowed to dispose of these as they pleased. Meggie sported several pretty buckles, after Davie started in the rag house.

It was back-breaking work—stooping most of the time for twelve hours a day.

'It stinks here,' said Johnnie.

'Aye, but we're paid to put up with it.'

Because of the through draft, they needed warm clothing, but the chief misery was fleas—fleas by the thousand, in every size, shape and colour, home and imported.

The kindly Jimmy, having started in the rag house himself, had known what it would be like, and had made it as easy as possible for the young lads.

To Sarah, he said: 'I must get a sack of salt for these two youngsters starting on Monday in the ragshop, I've told you what the fleas will be like.'

'Poor souls,' said Sarah, and sat deep in thought.

Later that night, she produced a huge, old sheet and, to her secret shame, spent the whole of the Sabbath making two pairs of dungarees and two dustcaps. 'Better the day, better the deed,' she thought.

Consequently, as Jimmy came off the nightshift on Monday morning, he met the two boys as they arrived. Under his arm were the two boiler-type suits, two caps and a large bag of salt.

'Now, Davie and Johnnie, listen to me carefully, My Sarah has made these overalls with tight legs, and two cotton caps for you. Take off your jackets and leave them in the cleansing room. Put on these garments and caps before you go into the flea-house. Sprinkle salt in any turn-ups or folds in cap and trousers. Dampen some salt and rub it along the seams and across the tops of your boots. Then, before you go home, strip and shake all your clothes outside—if you don't you will be carrying thousands of the wee buggers home with you—and put some salt in the corners of the blanket you sleep in. Remember, now, I have warned you.'

They took half-an-hour, that first morning, to get ready, then stowed the sack of salt in a dark corner for the next day. It made the job bearable. 'God bless Jimmy,' said John.

'And Sarah,' added Davie.

Instead, therefore, of carrying literally thousands of fleas to their respective homes, there would only be an odd few. Davie soon put salt on THEIR tails.

It was two proud youngsters who collected the three shillings and sixpence at the end of the week. They considered themselves well paid.

'Well, Davie, how is the job?' asked Neil.

'All right, except for the fleas, the place is fair hotchin with them.'

'Well, you must strip and wash at the pump in the yard and not bring them into the house, You can have threepence a week for yourself. See that you buy a penny packet of flea-powder.'

Davie did not mention the fact that Sarah had provided overalls and caps, nor that Jimmy had bought salt for them. His mother just assumed it all went with the job.

Fortunately, for Davie, this filthy job lasted only three months. As winter approached, one of the lads on the Kier left, and Davie moved to another building. Jimmy Geddes explained, 'The rags have to be cleaned, bleached and softened. We put them into this rotating boiler and we add two measures of this solution. We call this vat "the Kier". The boiler is allowed to rotate about fifteen hours for these coarse rags. The cleaner ones need six hours. You will have to learn how long to boil them, but I'll keep my eye on you. Just do as you're bid.'

Jimmy Geddes saw that he had a likely lad in Davie—and one with a bit of sense.

'You're very white today, lad, are you all right?'

'It's just the strong smell of caustic soda in the half stuff. I'll get used to it.'

The four shillings he now earned was vital to home-life. It paid for bread, milk and cheese for the whole family.

'Do you never have holidays like the school holidays?' asked Meggie.

'No, I would lose my money, Meggie, if I took holidays, but it will soon be the Fair and we can go on Saturday afternoon.'

'Can I bring my friend Mary, Davie? She is here for a few weeks.'

So it was, that Davie, Mary, Meggie and Willie went to the Fair in Blairton, the neighbouring market town, about five miles from Ruary.

None of the children had been to a Fair previously, so it was very exciting. Local farmers put benches in their carts and took family and friends to the Fair on Saturday. The children had been lucky and had managed to squeeze into one of the bigger carts.

Mary was Sarah's niece. She had been ill and, because she lived in a town, Sarah had brought her to Ruary for a change of air. Sarah loved children. It was so sad that she and Jimmy had none of their own. Jimmy had brought Mary down to the starting point and had said to Davie, 'Look after her, Davie, for me.'

'I will that.'

Mary came from a poor home also. She was the same age as Meggie and the two got on very well together. They had no money to spend on roundabouts or coconut shies, but it did not matter. They were content just to be there, so they walked round and round gazing at everything in wonder.

Sarah, the provider, had given Mary enough sandwiches and ginger-bread for all of them and money for lemonade. They all sat near the Punch and Judy and saw several performances. They were happy just to be there, watching. It never occurred to them that it was not hygienic for all four to be drinking from the same bottle. It was the Fair.

Every now and then, Davie felt in his pocket. Later on, in lordly fashion, this twelve year old asked: 'Would you all like a cornet?'

'But Davie, you are saving up for new boots.'

'Och, we will all have a half-penny cornet.'

All their lives they remembered Davie's generosity. To have vanilla ice-cream at Blairton Fair! The radiant smiles and the long, slow licking of the delicious ice-cream, each child trying to make his cornet last longest, was a sight indeed!

Years later, when Davie sat in a big hotel in Darjeeling eating ice-cream, it was Mary's, not Meggie's, face which floated before his eyes.

'Where do you live, Mary?'

'In Port-Glasgow, a long way from here—on the Clyde. I have been in hospital and I've come to stay with my Aunt Sarah, to get strong again.'

'Not Mrs. Geddes of Rose Cottage?' asked Davie.

'Yes, yes of course.'

Davie was astounded. He sometimes went to visit Jimmy and Sarah. This had begun when he went to thank Sarah for making the overalls and caps.

'Come any Sunday to tea, Davie, we would be pleased to have you.'

With just a little hurt in his voice, he said, 'Jimmy didn't tell me you were coming, but of course I have not seen him for two weeks. We are on different shifts.'

'Mary came unexpectely,' said Meggie, conscious that Davie was hurt.

'Yes, my aunt just came through to visit me and brought me back the next day. Uncle Jimmy did not know I was coming.'

'Sarah met me on the school brae and introduced us,' said Meggie, 'I was supposed to tell you, Davie, but I forgot.'

Davie was mollified. He considered Jimmy his best friend.

At thirteen, he was in charge of the dirty rag Kier and was earning four shillings and sixpence per week for twelve hour shift-work, but free from two o'clock in the afternoon on Saturdays.

3

'Now then, Davie lad, what is wrong this morning?'

Jimmy Geddes admired the pluck of the youngster for turning out. He could see that he was near collapse.

It was six o'clock in the morning on the dot and there was Davie struggling to empty the rag Kier. He was surrounded by clouds of steam and a strong smell of caustic soda. Davie looked as though he would gladly lie down and die. It was a cruel morning with deep snow and hard frost. Davie's tackety boots were 'letting in', they had been patched and re-patched. He was soaked to the knees.

'My mother is ill, father's on the bottle and Willie has 'flu. I haven't slept for three nights.'

This was a new departure. Neil could have a dram with the best of them, but 'to be on the bottle'.

This was when a flash of light blinded Jimmy Geddes—followed by long, slow anger, frustration, even contempt for Neil Cameron—all these bairns and he had started going to the bottle. What would he and Sarah not have given for just one child?

Indeed, at six o'clock in the morning in the Kier house, for the first time in his life, cautious, warm-hearted Jimmy acted on impulse and changed the course of three lives.

'Where do you all sleep, laddie?'

Davie's eyes filled with tears, which he manfully tried to hide. He was now fourteen, underfed, ill-nourished, ill-clad and worn out with responsibility which his father should have shouldered.

For the past two years, Sarah had given Jimmy too many sandwiches or pies for his meal break. When on the same shift he would find Davie and say, 'Drat the woman, she has given me too much again.' He would look at the boy's everlasting bread and dripping and say, 'I wish you would help me out, Davie, I dare not take it back and it is too good to waste.' Davie did not need to be asked twice; he wondered that Sarah was wasteful with such good food. Jimmy chuckled silently.

'The boys sleep on the floor,' he answered.

'Well, that is that,' said Jimmy to the painfully thin boy. 'You will just come with me right now, I'll see your father later.'

Jimmy went off to speak to the foreman.

'I'll be away for half-an-hour, Geordie. Tell the manager when he comes around and put one of the beatermen into the Kier house. Davie is ill.

In the past four years Jimmy had reached the giddy heights of becoming head foreman and felt justified in showing a little authority on this occasion.

With an arm around his shoulders, Jimmy propelled Davie out of the mill and up the short cut to his own little cottage.

'Sarah, I've brought you Davie, feed him and put him in the spare bed!'

'Laddie, you're all in. Drink this soup and get into bed.'

When the boy awoke it was black dark and he knew not where he was. Someone had put a lamp on the table, near his bed.

There was a tap on the door and Sarah said, 'Jimmy's orders—you are to eat every scrap of this, then go to sleep again.'

Davie looked wide-eyed at the plate of savoury meat and vegetables.

'Mistress Geddes, I'm sorry I cannot pay you for food like this, I've only threepence.'

'Later, you can work for the meat. Eat it!'

Several days afterwards, on recovering from utter exhaustion and hunger, Davie began to understand.

Since his family had left Inveraray nine years ago, he had received no such kindness. He had been the giver and the doer, even giving his last sixpence to a neighbour for bread.

Now, at fourteen, despite loving his mother, Davie had long felt concern, impatience, then anger and personal hurt against his parents—disappointment with his mother for putting up with things as they were. It seemed as though they could do nothing but produce babies, there were already nine of them and he was the eldest at fourteen. His mother's everlasting pregnancies wore her out and made her careless about food and cleanliness. She looked old at thirty-six. His father had lost heart, he spent too much of his twenty-five shillings and sixpence on drink now.

He did plant the vegetable garden and had it not been for this produce, they would have starved. The chickens at the far end of the garden were poor scrawny creatures with anaemic combs. They lived mostly on scraps from neighbours.

When Davie looked round this small, comfortable bedroom, so neat and fresh, disgust and rebellion rose within him. 'What good does my four shillings and sixpence a week do?' he thought.

He had carefully saved three shillings and sixpence for new boots before the winter came on. One Saturday he had taken the small tin from the top of the wardrobe, to find it empty.

'Mum, have you seen my boot money?'

'Yes, Davie, I needed it for coal, I am so sorry.'

He wondered if he was beginning to be disloyal. 'If father can drink as he does, I should have my sixpence per week for boots.' He could not help this thought, for his feet were always soaking wet and his chilblains red and painful.

Then again, 'If I got a job away, she couldn't do without my money.'

He was annoyed with himself for he no longer thought of mum and dad, not even of mother and father, but of 'he' and 'she'. This nagging feeling of slight criticism upset him—especially since the departure of Meggie.

A year ago, the postman had met Meggie on the hill.

'How old are you, Meggie?'

'Not yet twenty-one.'

'Seriously now, I might know of a good job for you.'

'Where?'

Near Inverness.'

'Inverness!'

'The laird's sister is here on holiday and she is looking for a "Tweenie"—honest, reliable, hard-working—the usual.'

With his heart as heavy as lead, Davie had accompanied Meggie to "Craigallion" up on the hill. Alice could not go, or was disinclined to make the effort.

'You are not twelve yet, Meggie. I don't think you should have to go so far until you are twelve.'

'Well, I'm eleven-and-a-half and by the time I get there I won't be far off twelve.'

'Remember now, Meggie, if you don't like Mrs. Anderson you are to open and close your left hand and then I will make some excuse for you.'

Clean and tidy, they presented themselves at the back door and were ushered into the kitchen. A supercilious footman was contacted. His open contempt and his icy 'Follow me' nearly rooted them to the spot.

'Two persons to see m'Lady.'

'Show them in. Oh Forbes, ask Mrs. Anderson to come down, please.'

Both Meggie and Davie had seen Lady Milne being driven through the village, but she was overwhelming at close quarters. Although well-scrubbed and tidy, the two children felt very much out of place.

Then Mrs. Anderson entered and this changed the whole atmosphere. She was friendly and charming, and put the two children at ease immediately.

'So you are Meggie, my dear, and you are . . . ?'

'Davie, m'am.'

'What lovely hair, Meggie, I declare it is truly chestnut.'

'How old are you?'

'rly twelve, m'am.'

'rather young to come as far as Inverness with me. Have you 'ference?'

'Yes, m'am, from the minister.'

'Well, this seems very satisfactory. You would work with the head housemaid in the morning and with the cook in the afternoon. I would give you an outfit of clothing plus your uniform and ten pounds per year. You would share a room with the under-housemaid.'

Meggie was tongue-tied but she was not moving her left hand.

'Because you are under twelve, perhaps I should see your mother.'

'Oh no, m'am. If Davie says yes, I will go with you.'

'Indeed!' Have you anything to ask me, Meggie?'

'Er . . . er . . . would I never be able to see my brother, m'am?'

Tinkling laughter. 'Of course, child. You are not coming to prison. I come here every summer for a month and you would come with me and, if your brother can save the fare, I would permit him to come and visit you.'

'Thank you, m'am.'

'What do you think, would you like to come? You will have to work quite hard, of course—up at six o'clock each morning. You may have one evening off each week, a half-day on Sunday and one day off per month.'

Meggie turned to look at Davie, her dark eyes asking THE question. Davie nodded.

'Splendid, I leave in a fortnight. Come and see me next Monday at three o'clock in the afternoon.

She rang the bell and said to the very superior footman:

'Forbes, ask Marion to take this child's measurements before she leaves, and see that she and her brother are given some lemonade and biscuits before they go.'

So, in a little pantry near the kitchen, Marion did just that. Meggie had to stand on a sheet of paper also, so that a line could be drawn round her feet, as a guide to shoe size.

Once outside the gates, both youngsters heaved a sigh of relief.

'I liked her, Davie, much better than Lady Milne.'

'Me too. At least you will have regular food and some good clothes.'

'Yes, and just two of us in a bedroom. There really is no room at home, Davie.'

'Hey Meg, do you realise that you are going to have as much money as I get, plus all your food and clothes!'

Davie was so relieved, although he could not think of Ruary without her.

I'll send you the fare from my savings, Davie.'

Meggie's eyes sparkled.

Two weeks later, he had said one evening, 'Goodbye, Meggie, I won't see you in the morning. Here is two shillings and sixpence I have saved for you, in case you need something.'

She hugged him and whispered, 'Thank you, Davie I love you best of all!'

He could not look at her. He just turned and ran to the mill.

'Even if I have to walk the seventy miles, I will see her when the mill closes for repairs,' he decided.

He worried about Meggie. She was so young and so far away. He wondered if she was lonely in the big house. He had heard how hard domestic service was. Mrs. Anderson had sounded quite a kind person, but one never could be sure.

'Well, Davie, I have spoken to your parents.'

Jimmy came into the bedroom, after work had finished. He and Sarah had said that Davie was to remain in bed for a few days.

'If you are willing, your father and mother will allow you to stay with Sarah and me. They agree that the house is overcrowded. You can have the attic here, all to yourself.

'My mother was willing?'

'Yes, Davie.'

'Sarah and I would be so happy to have you live with us.'

'But ... but ... my mother can't manage without my money, Jimmy.'

'There is to be a job on the beaters next week and I've spoken for you. You will soon be fifteen and that means a man's wage. The beaters are the most important section, so the pay is good. You would have twelve shillings and sixpence to begin with and when you have learnt the work, eighteen shillings. Very good for fifteen years old.'

Davie was almost speechless.

' ... my mother?'

'Well now, it's up to you, Davie. You will never get on if you get no sleep and little food. You are outgrowing your strength and if you go on to beaters it will be hard work. Sarah and I have talked things over and Sarah says she can keep you for seven shillings and sixpence. You can still take four shillings each week to your mother and you can have a shilling for yourself. Remember that your mother won't have to feed you—and Meggie also is away.

Davie went to see his mother. She was more than willing. She was well aware that Davie needed care. She could not feed him properly. His stomach just would not take the food she made. Also, it would make more room. Besides, he could come and see her often.

Neil was not very interested. 'Please yourself, Davie.'

So, on the following Saturday afternoon, Davie carried his few possessions along to the bungalow, having left four shillings with his mother.

As he appeared, Sarah went to the gate to meet him. 'Welcome, Davie, it's good to see you lad.'

They had waited for him to come to tea. Davie was fascinated by the food. Fish, home-baked bread, girdle scones and strawberry jam.

Sarah appeared very practical. She saw that it was an emotional moment for him.

'Well now, I've two men in the house, I'll sit back and do nothing.'

'You have a hope, Sarah.'

'Well, if Davie has any strength left after twelve hours on the beaters, he can hack sticks and carry coal for me.'

'See that you get pocket money for that, Davie . . . women!'

Now great tears dropped from the closed eyes.

'Thank you, Sarah, thank you, Jimmy, I'll try to please you.'

Sarah held out her arms and Davie had a long-forgotten motherly embrace.

'Come now, come now, none of this nonsense,' said Jimmy gruffly. 'I'll show you the attic.'

The room under the rafters seemed like heaven—a room to himself, an attic window overlooking the river and the woods, an iron-bedstead with clean white sheets and a patchwork quilt. A clothes cupboard and drawers stood along one wall and a dark-blue rag rug lay at the side of the bed on top of the blue linoleum. All for him!

He went to bed early. He had been sleeping on the floor for so long, he felt he was floating on a cloud.

The thought did cross his mind the following morning that his mother had not minded his going at all.

He really loved Jimmy and Sarah—in the same way that he loved Meggie. He took great pride in keeping his room spotless and showed his gratitude by helping Sarah in every possible way—by carrying the heavy basket of washing, by cutting sticks and carrying coal. On Sundays he came down early, lit the fire and made a cup of tea for Sarah. He had someone to care for and he was loved.

'I'm glad he is loyal to his mother,' said Jimmy.

'Yes, he takes four shillings each week and a bunch of wild flowers on Sundays.'

'I see you have wild flowers too.'

'Yes, I'm well content. I wish we had thought of this years ago.'

'It would not have worked then.'

Davie's hollow cheeks began to fill out and his eyes to sparkle. It was so good to have his clothes fresh and ironed, and his socks darned.

'Now, Davie, you must listen to me,' said Jimmy one Saturday evening. 'The manager says you can start on the beaters on Monday. I told him that, although you are a bit too young for the job, I had watched you for four years, that you work hard and that you have some common sense. You must understand that now you are entering the mill proper, for the first time, and if you listen now and then to what I tell you, you will soon get on in the trade. The beaters are the most important job in the mill—not the most difficult nor the most danger-ous, but the most important. I'll show you early on Monday morning.'

'You see this half-stuff, which you dealt with in the Kier, is dumped into this draining area. All the rags, by different preparations, are now snow-white 'stuff' which is led into the beaters—but here comes Joe the head beaterman.'

'Hullo, Davie, pleased to see you!'

'I'll leave him to you then, Joe. See you tonight lad.'

Joe showed Davie the correct consistency required of the 'stuff' and how, where and in what quantity to add colour.

'You think it is white, don't you?'

'Yes, Joe, it's white.'

'No, it is not a true white, you put in this measure of blue or sometimes of green to get the required white. Don't worry, it will take months to learn all the details. Because this is a high grade writing-paper mill, we nearly always have a beautiful white—but of course we sometimes have a true blue or lemon, or grey, but mostly white. Our particular paper is called "Silver Ripple" after the river. Jimmy will show you the watermark if you ask him.'

Davie was bemused. For years he had heard men talk in the village about 'Silver Ripple' and 'Silver Sheen' and here was the first stage in their production.

At 'home', as Davie had learnt to call 'Rose Cottage', Davie said to Jimmy, 'What lovely names, Ripple, Silver Ripple, Silver Sheen—I wonder why? I know 'Ripple' is from the river, but why the river?'

'Sir Geoffrey, the laird up in Craigallion, owns the mill and the river. The Ripple runs through much of his land.'

'OWNS the river?' asked Davie.

'Yes, and all the fishing rights, but he is a good master and for 500

28

yards either side of the hump-backed bridge, he allows the mill workers to fish or swim. Elsewhere is forbidden and I warn you that McCulloch, the ghillie, takes great pleasure in catching people who poach beyond the limit. If he calls in the law it can be imprisonment, but McCulloch is so fond of his whip it is usually a lashing.

'McCulloch,' shuddered Davie.

On the day that he was sixteen, Davie received his first ever birthday present—a warm pullover knitted by Sarah. He was touched and delighted.

'Straight home tonight, Davie,' said Jimmy, 'or the dumpling will get cold!'

'My, Davie, you're becoming a dab-hand on the beaters,' said his boss.

The boy glowed with pride. He felt so happy, life was interesting, he was a person, an individual with friends. He was so happy, also, to receive a letter from Meggie. They exchanged letters monthly and he had learnt that she was very contented in Mrs. Anderson's household. Davie need not have feared that she would be exploited, as in so many houses. She was coming down with her mistress for the month of June and what a lot they would have to talk about.

'You are too soft-hearted,' said Jimmy, one lovely Sunday in Spring. 'Perfect weather and you have no bike. It took you two years to save for a bike—and when you find a good second-hand one with rubber tyres, you give it to your brother Neil.'

'And you, Jimmy, are you not too generous?'

Jimmy grunted but he was annoyed for Davie's sake. The boy was cooped up all week in the fumes of the beater house and needed a spin in the country when he was free.

'Well, Neil is clever. The new headmaster said he should go to the academy in Blairton and he couldn't walk five miles each way, in all weathers. Besides, his friends cycle.'

'So Davie did without, again. I hope he appreciates it.' No response.

Davie's speech was becoming noticeably better. Sarah corrected him when she could. Having been brought up, until five, among Gaelic speakers, his grammar was fairly good, and he had retained the softly modulated voice.

'You must try to speak less of the Doric, Davie, if you are to get on in the trade,' she would say. She was ambitious for him.

'Did you learn to speak well when you were a nanny?'

'Yes, my job depended upon it.'

The remark brought back memories of long ago, when there had just been Meggie and himself. He must try to go back to Loch Fyne one day.

'I must speak like the men in the mill, Sarah.'

'Well yes, but leave it behind at the mill.'

'I have an aunt and uncle in Inveraray. They live on a croft.'

'Well, you ought to write to them and ask if you might visit them sometime, Davie. It is good to have relatives.'

'Do you ever hear from Mary? She and Meggie were good friends. Once we all went to the Fair in Blairton.'

'I have not heard for a long time. Jane, Mary's mother, has eight children and just does not have the time. Mary, I believe, is working in a dressmaking establishment. I must get her here again. She is a sweet girl.'

At seventeen, Davie was old in experience.

'Sarah, does life always go up and down like hillocks?'

Sarah, astonished, replied: 'Yes, Davie, it cannot be good all the time. When you are on the crest of the wave you have to brace yourself for a dip into the trough.'

'I have certainly come up from a long, deep one, thanks to you and Jimmy. We had to leave Inveraray because the English owner of the croft and smithy went bankrupt. My father heard about this black-smith's job at the mill so we came, but I often feel it was the wrong move. I've almost forgotten what the village and the loch look like.'

'You can take Jimmy and me there, when you are a foreman.'

Davie laughed aloud. It was as though he were learning what happiness was—a soft, ticklish feeling that welled up from toe to head, then a sudden release, in a burst of laughter.

Thus, in due course, Davie became head beaterman, with his one pound per week. All good things seemed to come together. June had arrived, sunny, with blue skies. The meadows were carpets of wild flowers. Children were making everlasting daisy chains and boys were messing about, under the bridge, in the river. But most exciting of all, was the arrival of Mrs. Anderson with Meggie.

Meggie was allowed to spend one week at Rose Cottage and every Saturday and Sunday. How she had grown! How pretty she looked! she was obviously well nourished and happy. She had fitted in very well to her new surroundings. She loved the work and its variety. When the family was out, she sang while about her duties. Her appealing brown eyes, added to a willingness to be helpful, had endeared her to Cook, who, despite the butler's rights, really ran the household.

'I'm a housemaid now, Davie, and Cook says I will get on well.'

In her free time, there was really nowhere to go at her age, so she 'visited' Cook in the kitchen and she learnt how to produce good and interesting food, which was to stand her in good stead in later life. Because Meggie was so young, sometimes on a free day, or if the family were not at home, Cook would take her to Inverness, or to visit her own family nearby. Indeed, there were many good people in the world, who really cared, thought Davie.

Sunday dinner at 'Rose Cottage' was a hilarious affair.

'We are amply repaid,' said Sarah, 'to have two such endearing young people looking on our house as their home.'

They visited Alice and Neil, of course, but there were still six children at home.

Willie worked for a local farmer and lived in. Neil was the brainy one. How he ever managed to do homework in that overcrowded house, Davie could not imagine. He had won a bursary to Blairton Academy and probably studied in a friend's house. He was a bit cocky, very sure of himself and seemed to have a photographic memory. Ishbel was nearly thirteen and was going into service soon—but the shock was that Alice was heavily pregnant again. Davie and Meggie just looked at each other. They delivered the cake and pies which Sarah had sent and they each gave Alice a few shillings for the children. They were silent for a time, then Davie said, 'It is early yet, let us go down by the river! Meggie, I feel disloyal, but does our father have no sense?'

'Mother looks terrible, Davie—so ill.'

'We shall just have to do what we can.'

'Mrs. Geddes, could I have Mary's address? We did write last year to each other but I've mislaid the address, she was the nicest friend I had.'

'Mary has been ill again and I have invited her to come for two weeks next month. Unfortunately, she cannot have free time before then. She is a dressmaker now, and doing well. I've sent her the money for the fare, she is the eldest of eight and there is little to spare.'

'What a pity it could not have been this month. I would love to see her.'

'We must try to arrange things better next year, God willing.'

As Davie took Meggie to Craigallion on the last day of her visit, they met Mrs. Anderson in the garden.

'You see, young man, I have taken good care of your sister.'

'Yes, indeed, m'am. I am most grateful.'

'Well, now you are old enough, you may come and spend two weeks with us at Ardmohr. Make the arrangements with your sister.'

Davie was overwhelmed. 'Thank you, I will try.'

July, also, was a happy month, for Mary did come to 'Rose Cottage' for nearly two weeks. Her visit added a new dimension to Davie's life. Fortunately, for the second week he was on day-shift and, as soon as the hooter sounded, he was out the mill gate like an arrow from a bow. It was even fun making up the sandwiches for himself and for Jimmy, and at midday she carried bottles of cold tea to the mill for them. They agreed that it tasted like wine.

Mary was good with children, so they took the young Camerons to picnic by the Ripple on a wide grassy verge. Sarah produced baskets of food, the sun shone, all the children were happy—there were cuts and bruises, young Tom fell into the water and had to be stripped. He went home wearing Davie's old pullover as trousers, his legs stuck through the arms. Laughter was the order of the day, as the group sat and played a short distance from the bridge.

'And what do you think you are doing here? Get out, the lot of you—double quick—poaching trout, I suppose.'

With a sick feeling in the pit of his stomach, Davie looked up and saw McCulloch, the ghillie, and his son Archie. For the last six years Davie had only seen Archie from a distance, their paths just did not cross very often. Davie had made it a policy to avoid the haunts of Archie—like the plague, not because he was a coward, but because he feared he might do Archie a mischief. Archie had also gone to the academy in Blairton and, unfortunately, was one of Neil's friends. They cycled together to school. That could explain, perhaps, why Davie was not over-fond of brother Neil.

Archie was tall, and built like a prize-fighter, but still wore that fixed, sneering smile of his childhood. As he looked at Davie, no longer gaunt and poverty-stricken, he smirked and puffed out his chest like a bantam cock. He was to go to college in the autumn.

'So it's you, auld pàtchie.'

Davie did not reply.

'Get out with your ragamuffin family—two minutes or I'll use the whip on you.'

Mary and Ishbel got the children out of the way.

'You are trespassing, so it is the law or the whip.'

Davie gulped. He was a young man of peace, in speech as in action, but he was also the man of the family.

'We are not trespassing, Mr. McCulloch. That great oak is the boundary and we are well within our rights.'

'I'll show you oak and rights,' thundered the ghillie, and raised his whip. As the whip fell, the tip of it caught Davie's ear, but it was changed days, he was now well-fed and strong and showed his mettle. He managed to catch the end of the whip and pull it from the unsuspecting ghillie—the most hated man in Ruary. He took one swing and, fortunately, he missed the ghillie but caught Archie across the thick-stockinged legs. The master-stroke was when Davie took the whip, coiled it, and threw it into the swirling water in the middle of the river.

'Now fetch the whip for your father, Archie!'

After a second's dead silence:

'The bloody nerve—you little b....... I'll teach you,' shouted McCulloch.

But Davie's luck held. Two men came strolling across the grass to see what the trouble was.

The McCullochs muttered something and strode off, but not before Davie had seen that Archie was as white as a sheet. He was a coward.

Back at Rose Cottage, Sarah and Jimmy looked grave, 'You did right, of course, Davie. Had you struck either of them with the whip, they would have had you for assault, but that devil will have it in for you from now on. Watch it. Avoid them, for the son is as sly as they come.'

Mary's last day had been ruined.

4

Davie had reckoned without Lisa—one of the maids at 'Craigallion'. She had been sitting on the other side of the Ripple with her boyfriend, and had seen and heard it all. With a few embellishments, she related the story to the cook and to the footman. Several of the staff remembered the incident of the patch, which at the time had been the talk of the village, and, in no time at all, the incident reached the ears of his lordship.

The laird sent for McCulloch, who was dumbfounded to receive orders to fix a neat board to the oak tree five hundred yards beyond the bridge.

'Private beyond this spot. Trespassers will be prosecuted'—and a similar board five hundred yards to the south of the bridge.

'By the way, McCulloch, I'm deducting the price of your lost horse-whip from your wages—there is no need to carry a whip while strolling on a Sunday afternoon.'

From that point on, Davie and Archie were sworn enemies.

Archie, the bully, had swaggered through school without opposition. The point was that the fellow did have brains, he was quick and intelligent but came of an uncouth father and a vociferous harridan of a mother. In the course of his seventeen years, he had been variously called Erchie, Archie, Arch—but now at the academy it was Archibald. that caused many a snigger in the village store.

Also, his father held a powerful position as the laird's ghillie. He was a good servant inasmuch as he protected his master's property extremely well, but Sir Geoffrey had no time for him as a man. He was kept in his service because he had poaching well under control. The villagers avoided crossing his path but the whole McCulloch family was extremely unpopular. There were two sly-looking, wispy daughters and, to overcome the ascendancy of the virago of the family, father and son bellowed and swore.

Archie still bullied most of the village youngsters. He had been taught how to box, so the lads avoided his punches when possible. He insulted and tormented the girls, therefore they gave him a wide berth.

McCulloch senior took special delight in stalking poachers and was universally disliked. He had had poor old Jake—a mentally handicapped man of fifty—sent to court for having caught a trout beyond the boundary. To save Jake from jail, there was a whip-round at the works to pay his fine. Had he been in Ruary, the laird would have quashed the whole affair. It was one more black mark against McCulloch and Co.

'I've tried so hard and so often to find one good point in the man, but I must be looking in the wrong direction,' confided Jimmy to Sarah.

Davie knew as much as anyone about guddling trout—he caught his first before he was five, in a burn running into Loch Fyne. He frequently caught fine trout in a deep pool in the Ripple just beneath the bridge. Indeed, while he lived at home, that was the one thing he enjoyed in the way of food. The chickens were never hung after their necks were wrung, therefore they were always tough. Indeed, he gave up eating chickens after coming in from school one day and seeing a cockerel, supposedly dead, get up and run out the back door after having been plucked. Meat, at that time of his life, was always boiled and stringy—but give him a trout grilled over a brander or out of doors—that made him drool. So, over the years in Ruary, he would guddle a trout either from the Ripple or from one of the many little streams flowing into it.

He knew of a good pool near the bank, just on the safe side of the oak tree. This particular Saturday evening, Davie and brother Willie were lying fully stretched on their stomachs, tickling trout—Davie half in the water and Willie leaning over the bank. They were competing and very intent on catching a fine specimen when, suddenly, splash!

'What happened Willie?'

There stood Archie, grinning from ear to ear.

'You're both poaching—that's your brother's and now for your fish, Cameron.'

With that, he hurled three beautiful trout into the middle of the river.

'I'll tell my father,' said Archie.

Willie swore, 'I'll get that bastard yet, you'll see.'

'You will do no such thing, Willie, you would be lashed. Let's play a trick on him.'

They knew that Archie would return, so Davie ran back to Sarah and asked for a few Condy's crystals. Willie had again caught three small trout. Loth to part with the precious fish, they nevertheless melted the crystals in a few drops of water and carefully dabbed the deep colour onto the fish. One they left on a stone in the middle of the Ripple, one in a tiny pool at the side, and the third caught in reeds well into forbidden territory.

'Let's hide behind the bush near the arch of the bridge and watch.'

They lingered an hour, and were just on the point of leaving, when Archie and his irate father arrived. McCulloch senior lifted the fish from the shallow pool.

'Ma conscience! It's a trout, but it's got the red disease. They found diseased trout last year in a burn near Pitlochry.'

Wringing his hands, he moaned, 'The laird is away, he's in London.'

'Then you must get his address from the house and send him a telegram.'

The culprits heard nothing of this, until Monday evening, when it was the talk of the village.

Somewhat discomforted, they feared they had gone a bit too far—but surely a man would recognise the colour and smell of Condy's crystals. However, they made a solemn oath to tell nobody at all.

A worried Sir Geoffrey arrived back on the overnight train from

London. Fish were taken from different burns and pools and tested. They were in perfect condition.

'You have been had, man,' he stormed, 'you are an incompetent fool. I've a mind to sack you.'

When she heard the tale, Sarah gave a sidelong look at Davie, but not even to Jimmy did she utter 'Condy's crystals'—but her eyes gleamed.

5

Davie was twenty and had been promoted to the machine house itself—regulating the feed coming from the beaters, so he was all the more surprised one evening when Jimmy said, 'You are doing very well, Davie, but it is time you had wider experience. As you know, we make very high grade writing paper here, but you must learn about newsprint, wrapping paper, esparto and woodpulp. These are coming things. Rags are getting fewer and the gypsies are not collecting as many for us. The day is not far off when it will be too expensive to make pure rag papers.'

Davie was shocked. He was beginning to feel comfortable and settled.

'You mean leave Ruary, Jimmy?'

'Yes, I do, if you wish to get on, and you cannot do that without varied experience. Sarah and I look upon you as our son and this will always be your home, but you do need a wider training. That was my own mistake in life. I stuck to rag papers. I will never be more than head foreman.'

Davie was silent.

'Don't look so downcast, you do not HAVE to go, now or ever, but I'm just thinking of your future.'

'But I have been only three months in the machine shop and I've only now mastered the fibre consistency.'

'You have learnt a lot, and very quickly, about beating and sizing. Some take years and some never learn about the uses of rosin, or alum, or casein, or china clay.'

Sarah looked near to tears.

'Let him be, for a few years, Jimmy, he has a lot to make up, in so many ways.'

'I'm only ambitious for him, Sarah. His field will be narrowed if he can only handle rags.'

'You don't mean that I have to leave home immediately?'

'Certainly not, never, if you so wish it. My thoughts are that our foremen are only in their thirties and forties. Unless one leaves unexpectedly, there will be no promotion here for many years. Whatever you decide, remember that this is your home and we want you.'

'Am I a nuisance to you, Sarah?'

'Heaven forbid that you should think so, Davie. It would break my heart to see you go.'

The seeds were sown. It took a lot of courage on Jimmy's part to do the sowing. He did not wish Davie to go away. The thought occurred to Davie often, that Archie and Neil had attended Blairton Academy all these long years, what an opportunity they would have in life. He must better himself.

He remained two more years as a machineman, then events made the decision for him.

A few months after this conversation with Jimmy, Davie's mother died. It was no wonder. She had had twins and they had died also. She died of sheer exhaustion at forty-three years of age, having given birth to twelve children. Although he still had love in his heart for her, he had lost much of the respect that is due to worthy parents. He thanked God that she was at peace, at last.

Neil had left the academy and had been offered an office post in Blairton. Ishbel and three of the other girls worked in a large clothier's and lived in. There were only four still at school. His father found a widow willing to act as housekeeper and look after the four school-children.

The young ones were strangers to Davie and Meggie. They never really knew them. What a life Alice had had! There should be a law against having so many children, when there was insufficient money to keep them fed and clothed. It had been a vicious circle—too many children—too much whisky—more children. The once handsome young father that Davie dimly remembered, was hard wrought and heartbroken.

The funeral was an agony for the sensitive Davie. Jimmy took the day off and did not leave Davie's side. Those black horses with nodding black plumes, that black vehicle with crêpe drapes taking away a young woman of forty-three—it was monstrous and so unnecessary.

Well, he had another home now and was deeply grateful for it. They could well manage at the cottages now. Davie felt as though a burden had been taken from his shoulders.

But a second event further delayed Davie's departure.

At twenty-two he was a young machineman. To a visitor the enormous machine, as long as a block of flats, with all its wheels and rollers, wires and felts, was frightening. The young men who mounted it to guide the new end of broken paper through to the rollers, were agile and sure-footed, but one day Davie was unlucky. Davie had had to work two successive shifts—twenty-four hours on end, among dangerous machinery, because his mate was ill. He was tired. The paper broke again and he had to climb up once more. He slipped and caught the fingers of his left hand in the huge rollers. The section was stopped but the damage was done. The two middle fingers of his left hand had been badly squashed—fortunately, on the first joints. Sick with pain, he was put into the manager's buggy and driven the five miles to Blairton to the doctor's surgery. It was an agony which took months to forget. There was no anaesthetic—bone splinters had to be removed as well as the nails, the flesh trimmed, cleaned and bound. The pain was so intense that, mercifully, he fainted. He was given a tot of whisky before being helped into the buggy.

Sarah and Jimmy, all concern, were awaiting him at Rose Cottage. He often wondered what he would have done without them. Had he been in rooms, it would have been a sorry story. No work, no money. He went to bed and stayed there for two days. He was exhausted, but after a week the pain became bearable. In his nightly milk, Sarah had laced a good measure of brandy. Sleep was anodyne.

'It is scandalous, there should be safety gadgets where the paper breaks, at least a handle to lean on or grasp with one hand. I am going to speak to the manager about it,' fumed Jimmy.

Meantime, Davie had been buying the 'Paper Trade Review' and had been discussing adverts with Jimmy. One appealed to him: 'Wanted, a machineman for a three machine mill in Lancashire ..."

'Apply for that, Davie. There you would get good experience in esparto grass and woodpulp papers.'

He left Rose Cottage heavy-hearted and lonely. He would rather have stayed and remained a machineman for life he thought. He was walking away from the only real adult love he had known, and Davie needed to be loved.

'Come home the first week-end you can get, Davie,' said Sarah as she kissed him goodbye.

'Be sure to write to us often.'

'Yes, Jimmy. Thank you both for all your love and care.'

For eighteen months he lived in a bedsit above a grocer's shop in a dismal town in Lancashire. His good references from the manager at Ruary had got him the job and he knew that he had to stay there for a time, but he hated every minute of it. He would look out on a foggy day and think of 'dark satanic mills'. He made acquaintances but no intimate friends, but he bit his lip and got down to the job of learning different methods, using mostly woodpulp and esparto grass, sometimes with a few rags plus the recycling of vast quantities of waste paper. He learnt when to use certain alkalis, how to get rid of linseed oil or ink and when to use mechanical and chemical pulps.

During 'Wakes Week' Davie went home to Rose Cottage to a great welcome. There was a change in Sarah, but she was as loving as ever.

'Sarah is very breathless going upstairs, Jimmy, I had not noticed it before.'

'It began recently, the doctor says that her heart is not so good. She must slow down a bit.'

'Now, Davie, you must not spoil me. I'll miss you too much when you go back.'

After the seemingly everlasting mist or fog to which he had become accustomed, the pure air of Ruary was a tonic.

While Jimmy was at work, he and Sarah strolled along the riverside, they sat in the garden while Davie practised the birdsongs again and he was thrilled to have a conversation with a thrush, repeating its notes over and over again. Davie would have liked to think it was his old friend of the woods singing in recognition.

How he hated the grimy city. His whole being was in tune with the countryside—to hear a curlew call, to see a trout jump, was bliss. It was even good, just to keep on digging in Jimmy's garden.

That winter, Sarah died. She had seemed to recover from a nasty, feverish cold, but one day her heart just stopped. Jimmy found her sitting in the big armchair in the kitchen, on his return from work. His Sarah had left him.

Davie asked for a week's leave and rushed North.

'I came at once, Jimmy. How are you?'

He did all he could to help but what good were words? Already Rose Cottage was strange, although Sarah's presence was everywhere.

'Will you stay on in the cottage, Jimmy?'

'Aye, Davie. I'm sixty-two now and getting tired. The Widow

Clelland will come and 'do' for me. I'll just exist until it is time to join Sarah.'

'She was a mother to me, Jimmy. I, too, loved her dearly.'

Indeed, Davie's heart was very heavy. He felt Sarah's loss much more than that of Alice. Strange, he thought, how some people radiate love. He would always believe that she had saved his life.

'Goodbye, Jimmy, I hate to leave you, but I'll be up again in the summer, so keep the fire burning.'

'I'll look forward to it, lad.'

But it was not to be. When the telegram arrived, Davie did not need to open it. Its very weight was leaden.

Jimmy having gone, Davie had no real link with Ruary. He went to another funeral. Three in two years. He was really depressed. Now he and Meggie were truly alone. While in Ruary, he paid duty visits to his father and stepmother—for Neil had married his housekeeper. His father seemed to have pulled himself together and the house was tidier.

Rose Cottage had only been rented, but Sarah and Jimmy had left him their personal possessions and two hundred pounds—a fortune indeed. How hard they must have saved to have that sum to leave. They worked so well together, thought Davie, that is the secret.

'I'll never go back,' he thought, on returning to his job. 'I could not bear it.'

A few months later, he applied for a job as Head Machineman in Rawnpore Mills, Bengal, and sailed from Southampton one September morning when he was twenty-four years of age—into the unknown, but an experienced papermaker, 'honest, reliable and a capable charge-hand,' said one of his references, 'and experienced in all types of papermaking.'

While in Lancashire, he had paid a schoolmaster two-shillings-and-sixpence per lesson to teach him all about decimals. He always felt he had missed out on this, because of his sudden departure from school.

He set sail with suitable clothing for India, the 'Complete Works of William Shakespeare', the poems of Robbie Burns and Sarah's Bible. He wore Jimmy's gold watch and chain and he had two hundred pounds in the bank for emergencies.

But there was no-one on the dock to wave him good-bye, nor to wish him well. He was alone again.

6

He was a good sailor—only slightly queasy in the Bay of Biscay. The firm was paying his expenses, of course—second class. He shared a cabin with a young subaltern who was returning, after his first leave home, to India. Davie was regaled with tales of Army life and social pleasures in the hill stations. It was all very amusing; that was how the other half lived and it was fun to listen to the amorous experiences of this young soldier. At the back of his mind, Davie was well aware that such an interestingly boring life was not for him.

Davie was no puritan. After he had been rescued by Jimmy and Sarah, he had learnt to love life and laughter, but the grind of poverty and ill health in his childhood had left its scar. When most people were in their cabins in the Bay, he had time to sit and reflect.

He was so pleased and happy for Meggie, who, at twenty-two, had married the son of a prosperous farmer in Aberdeenshire. It had happened quite suddenly. Meggie, too, had 'improved herself'. She had become personal maid to Mrs. Anderson and was well liked in that household. While accompanying Mrs. Anderson to a wedding in Ellon, she had met Peter Munro and fallen head over heels in love with him. Just as Davie was preparing to leave Lancashire he received a letter from Meggie: 'Dearest Davie, I've fallen in love and I'm to be married, in Inverness, to a farmer from Ellon, on the twenty-fifth of July. Please come, Davie, and give me away.'

So, spending hard earned pounds and sitting four hours on hard, third-class, wooden seats, he travelled all the way to Inverness, approved the quiet, clean-cut young farmer, who was to be his brother-in-law, and saw Meggie starry-eyed and happy. He was proud of her and she of him, and she was so very pleased that Davie really liked Peter.

'Davie, we only have each other as family, apart from Peter I mean, so we must keep in contact—close contact. Let us write regularly and we can share in each other's news and lives.

'Yes, I promise.'

Meggie would be all right. He must remember to send a card to her from each port of call. 'Life must have a plan,' he mused. The very fact that he felt ready to go abroad, indeed had made plans to do so, just when Meggie decided to get married. How could he have left her, virtually alone.' At one point, he even thought of taking her with him, but conditions at Rawnpore were unknown to him, and he realised that the climate would be unsuitable for women and children. Things had worked out very well and Peter had repeated: 'Make this your home, Davie, when you come back on leave.' Yes, Meggie was lucky.

When they arrived in the Mediterranean, he went ashore with a group of young people at each port of call. He had, however, sense enough to decline personal invitations from mamas with young daughters. As he sat thinking, he could hear Sarah's voice: 'Now Davie, walk tall but know your limitations, you still have a lot to learn.' True, he thought, knowing how to handle decimals makes me no savant. He was so grateful to Sarah also, for making him speak the King's English, although he never did lose the lilting cadence of his Highland forebears. Of that, he was secretly proud.

He surveyed all the young ladies on board, with a cool eye. He measured them all physically against Meggie and Mary, and behaviour-wise against Sarah, who remained endearing to the end.

So, in the Mediterranean ports he preferred to accompany the quieter, less sexy types. He avoided the beauties so obviously in search of a husband. Jimmy had said more than once: 'Davie, ladies and gentlemen are born not made by material success, remember that all your life.'

Davie was indeed a born gentleman, in looks and in manner. About five feet eleven inches, with fair, curling hair and deep blue eyes which one trusted on sight, but he was no saint.

He thought again of Ruary and, inevitably, of the family McCulloch. How odd it was that the men brutally, and the women bitchily, had harassed the whole village. A few young men, himself included, ought to have taken a stand and had a real battle with Archie and his father. Having had to work such long, hard hours, they had been literally too tired to do it. They just hoped that the McCullochs would fade away. Nobody had dared complain to the laird; they feared loss of work in the mill. The local policeman was McCulloch's cousin, so he was no use. Yet, the poor folk of Ruary had had their own method of retaliation. Davie smiled at the memory.

Some wag, on the weighing machine in the rag-shed at the mill, had told the gypsies that they could save themselves several miles by taking the short-cut past the McCullochs' house and along the path at the foot of their garden. This was a right of way, he said. For years afterwards, the McCulloch family had to chase gypsies out of their garden. Often, vegetables and chickens disappeared with them.

Then there was the time that Davie's mate in the rag-sorting shed, had been caught by McCulloch's whip as he was carrying a rabbit, snared, of course, but not on the laird's land. He and Johnnie thought long and deeply:

'Let's plague the bastard,' said Davie. 'you know that we can't light a fire in the woods, but what is to stop us carrying half-burnt sticks and charred paper well past the oak tree . . . '

'And what possible good could that be, you ass?'

'Listen,' said Davie. 'When the tinkers bring the next load of dirty rags, we will not take off our overalls before leaving. We shall be hotchin' with fleas.'

'You're a fool, Davie, we would be the sufferers.'

'Wait a minute, we could run to that great stone slab near the tree, strip and shake our overalls and caps. We could collect dozens of fleas, hundreds even, and put them into two empty matchboxes.'

'Go on, you're not so daft for twelve years of age.'

'Then we make a circle of stones, lay the charred paper and sticks and leave the two closed matchboxes beside them. McCulloch and Archie always pass the spot on the way home. It's summer and not too cold. We could climb two trees and wait and see what happens. Just don't fall down or even sneeze.'

Involuntarily, Davie smiled again when he thought of the nerve of it—Johnnie up an oak, but not THE oak, Davie hidden in a great spruce. Both boys had pieces of cloth pushed into their mouths, as gags, in case they burst out laughing.

Along the pine-needle path, cracking his whip, and as usual accompanied by Archie, came McCulloch. With a great oath, he pointed to the signs of the fire.

'The varmints, the bastards!'

'The bloody fools forgot to take away their matches,' piped Archie.

Simultaneously, they each lifted a matchbox and opened it. The confined and frantic fleas, with one mighty leap, landed on face, neck, hair and burrowed under shirt and coat collars, not to mention the more private areas.

'The bloody devils. I'll have the law on them for this.' The mighty Archie stood and wept.

Trained in a hard school, the two culprits knew that their very lives depended upon their silence. For weeks afterwards, they could not meet each other's eyes in public.

When Mrs. McCulloch asked Alice when Davie had arrived home that night, Alice answered in all innocence, saying: 'The same time as usual. About half an hour after the whistle blew.'

In later years, when Davie told Sarah of the escapade, she nearly tied herself in knots with laughter. Sarah really was a good sport.

When Johnnie and Davie later went to the Fair, they visited the flea circus, but it was tame compared with their own efforts.

'A penny for your thoughts, Mr. Cameron,' said Deborah. Davie gulped, thinking, 'if only she knew.'

'Oh, DO tell,' she purred. But that was hardly possible.

Miss Deborah Hawkins was going out to join her parents in Delhi and was duly chaperoned by elegant Mrs. Dennison, wife of an Army officer. The latter was so correct and precise. Davie, highly sensitive, was aware of a certain condescension.

At concerts on board ship, Davie, cajoled by the kittenish Deborah, made a great hit by his imitations of bird songs. He whistled in wistful memory to his old friends of Ruary—the mavis, the blackbird and the skylark. His repertoire seemed endless.

'Why don't you come to the ball tonight, Cameron?' said Sub-Lieutenant Crawley—'great fun, lots of girls, and pretty too.'

'They are all right, but I won't be patronised.'

'You go ashore with some of them.'

'Yes, but I don't dance.'

It's a pity really, thought Davie, thinking of his very light-weight Cameron kilt and the linen jacket and lace ruffles which had been his one extravagance in clothing. He had, of course, worn the kilt with a velvet jacket at Meggie's wedding. He had looked very handsome in it, so everyone said, and Meggie had whispered, 'I'm very proud of you Davie,' and he had whispered back, 'And I of you.'

However, he had never learnt to dance. In his early years, it had taken all his energy to survive and to be fit for the next day's grind, plodding wearily to and from the mill gates. Physical energy apart, when he was young, his parents had still retained their puritanical outlook. Cards were forbidden, cards implied gambling and gambling was the work of the devil. As for dancing, that was even worse.

Because he had delivered groceries for her in the snow, old Mrs. Niven of Ruary corner shop, had given him a pack of cards and an ancient phonograph with a few wax rolls of music. One evening he Meggie and Willie had been playing snap, when his mother had come in, taken one horrified look at their game, scooped up all the cards and thrown them in the fire. She then turned and saw the phonograph; she seized it and hurled it on to the cement at the back door. It shattered into a hundred fragments.

'How dare you, Davie! No child of mine will bring either the voice or the work of the devil into this house. Put every scrap of it into the ash-box.'

The children were terrified and shrank into a corner of the room. With supreme self-control for a boy of twelve, Davie said not a word, but he was horrified at the unreasoning fury on his mother's face. Later, he realised that that was the point when he first felt critical of his parents' outlook and way of life. What harm had he done? He worked so hard, tried to be so helpful, and he was permitted no single pleasure. He became withdrawn and more silent than ever.

Sarah was so different. She would have said, 'Isn't it a wonderful invention—such fun, just don't play it on a Sunday.' Davie would have respected that. Indeed, he often went to Church with Sarah. He did not much care for the preacher, who was inclined to thump the pulpit and preach hell-fire and brimstone, but he loved the old Scottish Psalms. Even as a youth, he had a firm, unshakeable belief in God, but found Him among the trees when he was alone by the river or when the lark rose soaring from the meadow, then did deep call unto deep. He retained a strong sense of the spiritual all through his life, but he did not talk about it, rather did he act in accordance with this deep, inner source of strength.

So, even while at Rose Cottage, there had been neither time nor energy to learn to dance—not even the Scottish reels, but their tunes always made him tap his foot and hum.

However, this voyage was to last more than four weeks, and a certain little widow, at least ten years older than Davie, had been straight and frank.

'Mr. Cameron, four-and-a-half weeks is a long time on board ship, and after Aden we have no port of call before Bombay, so do come and stretch your legs. I will teach you to dance.' She added mischievously, 'I assure you, I have no ulterior motive.'

She was a delightful person, a good companion and interesting to talk to. She had no trap set for a handsome young Scot but wished to have a pleasant friend en voyage. She was taking an elderly lady out to join her son in Poona, and became bored at times. She and Davie became firm friends.

So, firstly on deck, when nobody was about, Davie learnt to waltz, to dance the valeta, the military two step and some of the reels and folk dances.

Gradually, he was persuaded to join thé dansant and finally the evening ball. The first evening, when he appeared in his kilt and ruffles, he was lionised. Being just Davie, he was acutely embarrassed and retreated for a while with the young Mrs. Reed to the nearest bar. However, he was a born dancer, as she repeatedly assured him, so light on his feet and he was adept at all the latest dances, before they reached Calcutta.

'Where DO you hide, Davie?' purred Deborah.

'Mostly in the library. I enjoy reading.'

'How very dull,' she said, pouting.

'If only she knew,' thought Davie, 'that I never had a chance to read until now.' He read avidly—all sorts of books; it was as though he was obsessed by the feeling, that he must try to make up the years of schooling which had been denied him. Towards the end of the voyage, one day in the ship's library, he found an old book, 'History of Papermaking'. He borrowed it and was thrilled to discover that it dealt with papermaking in ancient times. To think that paper had been handmade two thousand years ago by the Chinese, then by the Arabs who had taken Chinese prisoners in Samarkand and learnt the secret. Through the centuries, what a fascinating role had been played by the Persians using flax and later rags, the Greeks, Moors, Italians, French, then the British. That rag paper was mentioned in the twelfth Century tract of the Abbot of Cluny, that watermarks were known from 1293, Davie could not put the book down. He was enthralled by the mine of information. To think that, as dirty little urchins in the rag shed at Ruary, he and Johnnie had been recent links in the long history of paper. It gave that filthy flea shed a new status, albeit an unsalubrious one. The very name of Samarkand thereafter sounded like music in his ears.

Not having finished the book by the end of the voyage, he asked if he might borrow it, promising to send it back to the ship when finished.

'I'm sure we would be pleased to be rid of it, sir. It is not even in the catalogue and is on our list for discarding. Do us the favour of keeping it.'

Well, it was like a gift of gold to Davie, who treasured it all his life.

Deborah was a beauty in a sensuous way—having a mass of redbrown hair framing her pretty face, 'painted' lips, and a touch of rouge. All this did nothing to improve her in Davie's eyes, nor did her low-cut apple-green gown, which was highly provocative. Davie was not seriously tempted—a good-night kiss, as with several other pretty girls after the ball, was enough for him.

He had sent several cards to Meggie and Peter, usually ending 'Regards to Mary' but he did not have her address.

'I wonder what has happened to her,' he thought frequently, 'we were twin souls.'

So they proceeded through the Suez Canal and the Red Sea, with fans but no air-conditioning; it was too hot even to flirt!

Davie slept on deck with a few other young men, but chaperons made sure that the girls suffered the heat in the confines of their cabins.

He had accompanied Deborah, Mrs. Scott and others on a tour of Port Said and of Aden, but the towns were so hot and dirty, and they had been warned not to eat fruit or drink water; so they were glad to return on board to enjoy long, cool drinks.

It had been amusing to watch little boys dive for coins in the harbour. They swam like fish. Their elders buzzed around the ship in small boats trying to sell their wares. In the Red Sea, it was fiendishly hot. Davie wondered what the temperature would be in the machine house at Rawnpore.

'Hot, huh?' said his cabin companion. 'Coming to dinner?'

'Of course, I am used to heat,' said Davie.

In after years, he realised that, during that long voyage to India, he had matured greatly. He had seen and learnt a lot, had avoided the 'bright set', made a few pleasant acquaintances and had learnt when to remain silent, when he felt ignorant about the point under discussion.

By the time the ship was nearing Calcutta, he had a notebook full of addresses—mostly in the fashionable hill stations, where he would be received by doting mamas.

'Hmm, if only they knew,' he would chuckle to himself. 'I would be ostracised. I'm no catch, by a long chalk.' Then again, 'I must stop thinking "if only they knew". The fact is, that they don't know the difficulties of my childhood. All that is in the past. Now only the present and the future matter.'

7

After Calcutta, there was a hot, slow, overcrowded train journey for one hundred and fifty miles to Rawnpore. Even travelling first-class, the carriage was like an oven. The train was so overcrowded. Natives were sitting on the roof, hanging out of the third-class windows and from anywhere that provided a foothold or a handhold. Now and then, he felt a bit apprehensive, this huge country was so different in every way from anything he had ever known. But again, at such times, he thought of Sarah, who, when Davie was diffident about some new venture, would whisper 'Walk tall, Davie, walk tall!' Once again he thought, 'Dear Sarah, how much I owe you! You were always an ally.' The beautiful flowers by the side of the track reminded him of bees. Sarah and bees!

Jessie McCulloch, Archie's mother, had met Sarah at the corner shop about a year after Davie had gone to live at Rose Cottage.

'It's a good thing I like cooking,' laughed Sarah, 'my men have such big appetites.'

'Well if you will take in ragamuffins, what can you expect?'

Mrs. Niven intervened: 'Have you seen the new vegetables, called tomatoes, Sarah?'

Sarah's eyes gleamed. 'No, but ragamuffins wouldn't miss tomatoes, never having seen them.'

A few days later, there was a swarm of bees from Jimmy's hives. Jimmy was at work, so Sarah donned overall, trousers, boots, hat, veil and gloves.

'Davie, fetch the big, empty jampot from the cupboard!'

With great care and much patience, Sarah got the Queen Bee into the pot. Sparks showering from her eyes, she asked, 'Davie where would you like to put her?'

'Best you don't know where, Sarah. Just give me the Queen.'

It was late afternoon when he reached the McCulloch garden. The horse and trap were not there, so they had gone shopping in Blairton. Davie sauntered jauntily past McCulloch's barking cur and shouted, 'Anyone at home?'

What he would have done, had anyone replied, he did not consider. Fortunately, there was no reply. He carefully opened the jar and tipped the Queen Bee through the half-open kitchen window. Bees which had followed him were there in no time at all and before Davie could say 'damn it' as he was stung on the leg, there were dozens of the things flying through the open window. Then he was off like a hare through a hole in the hedge and along the back path, whence he had come. All Sarah said was: 'What's wrong with your leg, Davie?'

'Oh, I was stung when I was in the field, on my leg and on my hand.'

'Get out the baking soda, lad, and I'll see to you.'

Sarah had no idea where the Queen Bee had been placed until the next call at the corner shop.

'Wasn't that just terrible for Jessie McCulloch?'

'What was?'

'When they got back from Blairton on Saturday, bees had swarmed in her kitchen. McCulloch took all night to get the place clear of them, then the kitchen was full of smoke and now Jessie has to wash the walls down. She had just done her spring cleaning too.'

'Oh dear,' said Sarah. 'She must have left a window open, when she went out.'

It now occurred to Davie, halfway between Calcutta and Rawnpore, that, although the McCullochs had ruled Ruary by brute strength and the whip, they had been amply punished by the subtlety of the villagers. Unlettered brains had outshone brawn over and over again. In fact, at this distance, Davie felt a little sorry for them, they had so many enemies in the cottages.

At last, the long journey was over.

'Are you David Cameron?'

Davie stood on the tiny platform at Rawnpore, his large tin trunk beside him and a grip in his hand.

'I am Alan Turner—your opposite number. Welcome to Rawnpore! I have a ghari here for your luggage and a small ekka for us.'

Davie was delighted to see a young man of about his own age, who smiled at him cheerfully.

The heat was intense. Two young porters lifted the trunk into the ghari, then the two vehicles moved off.

The mill lay about five miles away, on the Ganges.

'This is the Burra Bungalow for the younger men, the one opposite for more senior men. The two bungalows to the right are married quarters, the larger bungalow to the left is for the manager and the really long place at the far end is retained for the managing director or other V.I.P.s. That, Cameron, represents the white population of Rawnpore.'

Trees surrounded the compound—mainly mangoes—and in the centre there was a small lawn surrounded by flowers.

'I did not expect to see a garden with flowers in this area,' said Davie.

'We do our best to maintain it. But all the water has to be brought from the river. In a very hot season we give up, I fear, but it is our pride and joy and we do try to keep the flowers alive. The bungalows are clustered together because we are within a few miles of the jungle and it makes for safety. Sit here on the verandah, in the shade, Davie, and I'll bring you a long, cold drink. Then you can have a bath.'

Davie relaxed, he felt he had found a friend. Indeed, they became friends for life.

They had so much in common, although Davie found that, despite his many difficulties, he had been the better off. He had been loved by Meggie, Sarah, Jimmy and, for a while, by his mother.

It always amazed him that Alan was such a loving and compassionate person, never having known love. Much later, Davie learnt that Alan had spent twelve years in an orphanage and life had been raw in the extreme. It was not run by the state but by a charitable organisation and they were never allowed to forget it.

'Why didn't you tell me long ago that you were an orphan?'

'I resent pity and I have told nobody else. So, please honour my confidence. Now that I've made the grade, I don't feel so bad. I'm a whole individual and independent.'

'Did you never know your parents?'

'No. I was illegitimate, and you know the disgrace that is held to be. Sins of the parents visited on the children. I was abandoned when I was about a week old and was lucky to be found and taken to an orphanage. I was named after the policeman who found me—Turner— and Matron consulted her alphabetical list and came up with the name Alan, so there it is. We were creatures of charity—poor food, little of it, and until I was five I usually had to wear girls' cast-off dresses. Very few boys' garments arrived at the institution. We lived cold, and worked from seven years of age. Some worked in mines or in factories. I was one of the lucky ones. I can draw a bit and I was sent to the porcelain factory and learnt to paint designs and figures on china—the cheaper variety. I received sixpence per week which was handed over to the matron, but at least I went out in trousers. When I was twelve, the factory closed and I was sent to the paper mill. Here I am.

'Lucky that you lived in the Midlands and not in Scotland!'

'Believe me, Davie, it can be bitterly cold in the Midlands, with soot and freezing fog. The workers were good to me. They often gave me a crust or a piece of cheese—or any food they could not finish! Matron was a good woman, really. No doubt it was very difficult for her to support the number of children she had to care for. There were fifty when I was there. Life was so regimented. We always seemed to be lining up to march somewhere or other. Disobedience brought dire punishment, but I shall always remember one kindness she meant to do me. I had been very ill with pleurisy and was very slow in recovering. The coarse food just revolted me, so one day Matron slipped up to my bed carrying a small box filled with sticky home-made toffee. She offered me quite a chunk. Of course, I thanked her, but was nearly sick—the poor old girl had cut the toffee with an onion-flavoured knife. I had no way of getting rid of the mouthful and sucked it like medicine. She retired soon after I left, but I did visit her once or twice. She was the nearest thing I had to a relative.'

When he met someone who had been more wretched than himself, Davie always felt guilty—he had had Meggie, Sarah and Jimmy.

'You know that your secret is safe with me, here is my hand on it.'

Alan and Davie had rooms near each other in the Burra Bungalow. The third machineman was married to a Eurasian girl and lived in one of the small bungalows.

'I'll show you round tomorrow, Davie, have a good rest and remember always, without fail, to let your mosquito net down, even if you are only having a midday siesta. The mosquitos here are vicious. Also, never go into the sun without wearing your topee.'

Everything was so new and so strange. All the furniture was made of bamboo and each piece was set on special metal blocks to prevent the ants eating through the wood. Next to the bedroom was the bath with a primitive douche. The toilet was outside, but had a door leading into the bedroom. Each little flat had a small cupboard to hold bottles and tinned food, and a further tiny cupboard lined with metal to house the daily supply of ice.

'The firm keeps us in ice, Davie—a large block each day—shout long and loud if it is not delivered. It is your survival line in the hot season.'

On the verandah and in the sitting room were punkahs, and one servant sat underneath pulling the rope to make a breeze.

In the Burra Bungalow there was a communal dining room. Four natives cooked in turn for the sahibs. The mill, of course, ran twenty-four hours per day, five-and-a-half days in the week. Because of shift work, breakfasts, lunches and dinners were often being served at the same time.

'Keep your private supplies locked up, Davie, in the bigger metal-lined cupboard. Supplies come only once a month from Calcutta, we send the list down at the beginning of the month and it is delivered about the third week.'

The salary was two hundred pounds per annum, of which one-third was paid into a British bank of their choice. The accommodation and basic meals were the perks. Luxuries had to be paid for extra.

'I suppose when supplies run short there are a few borrowers around.'

'Exactly, especially with the drinks. By the way, I have a very good bearer, honest and very reliable. He asked me whether you would care to employ his brother. They are twins and would like to be together. Ram and Asi Singh, they are called.'

'Bearer?'

'Yes, you need someone to do the chores for you, to see that the dhobi does your clothes on time, and to look after your property in general. Remember that you will need at least three changes per day when you start in the mill. Believe me, after you have done a six hour stint in the machine house, you will need to be helped up the bungalow steps.'

So it was, Alan became Davie's friend and mentor, and Ram became his faithful bearer.

'We get up at four o'clock in the morning, have a game of tennis, bath, then get down to the works.'

'Tennis? I have never played tennis.'

'Nor had I, until I came out a year ago. You must learn, I will teach you. You would go to pot without exercise. Watch the older men, lots of them are on constant brandies and sodas, and are fat and liverish. Besides, we need any interest we can find here. Life is very monotonous.'

So, the first list for Calcutta was made out. Alan suggested a few specialities—tins of bacon, of sausages, of fish, of corned meat, three bottles of whisky, plus dozens of bottles of light ale.

'I don't drink. I have never been able to afford it.'

'After an exhausting day, you will need a tot of whisky and you will have friends to entertain.'

Tennis clothes, racquet, balls, playing cards, were also added to the list.

At the word 'cards' Davie faltered.

'Do you play for money, Alan?'

'If we do, it is only for farthings. There are a few gamblers. Avoid them like the devil.'

Entering the mill was like entering an oven, quite literally. Every door and window was open, but air-conditioning was unknown. Davie gasped. He would never stand this, he thought, looking at the enormous machine. Ah well, he had come on six months trial, he would go back to Ellon after that and be a farm-labourer. Why had he come? To make a little money? For experience? A sense of adventure? In his position, it was the only available way of seeing the world.

The white men worked from half-past six until half-past eleven in the morning, returned to the Burra Bungalow for lunch and a siesta, then went back to the mill from three o'clock until half-past six in the evening. That was the day shift.

For the first few weeks, Davie could scarcely eat. Cold, iced beer was what he craved for. Now he understood why the men who had been here for years, without wives or families, took to brandy. But he would be away in six months, leaving his damned tennis racquet behind him.

Sundays were bliss. On Saturday afternoons and Sundays, the engineers did the repairs—a very skilled job on such intricate machines. He found the other machinemen and engineers very decent fellows. It was quite a cosmopolitan community and each individual just had to get along with his companions.

They made their own fun. On Sundays, a group of them would go, either on horseback or in ekkas, to the local bazaar. They frequented one particular fruit stall. It belonged to the bearers'—Asi and Ram Singh—cousin's cousin. The owner had been well tipped and, with a friendly smile and sparking eyes, promised by all he held sacred 'to sell only fruit as it grew on the tree'. Alan had seen the dire consequences of eating fruit injected with contaminated water and sold by budmarsh vendors.

'In the mill, only drink water from the sealed bottles, Davie!'

'To think, I just used to cup my hands and drink from the burn at Ruary.'

'Coming to the dance tonight, Davie?'

'Dance? I thought we were on the edge of the jungle.'

'Yes, but five Koss, which is two miles, down river, the people at the jute mill are having a 'do'. The manager has twin daughters who are twenty-one today and both very pretty, so most of the boys will be going.'

Saturday night, dark-blue clouds with a huge silvery moon, and seven eligible batchelors in two ekkas made for a lively drive down river. They would spend the night on the jute compound and drive back in daylight.

'It is eerie to hear the peculiar animal sounds from the woods,' said Davie.

'Oh, you will soon get used to the hyenas and to the monkeys, but NEVER go out at night without two servants with lanterns and pronged sticks—because of snakes.

Davie thought, 'One month gone and five to go.'

Surely he could not lose still more weight in the heat of the machine shop—he was gaunt already. The weekends were like oases in the desert.

At the jute mill the reception was hearty. The drinks were cool and, thanks to his lady friend aboard ship, Davie could dance well. The twins were charming, but not as pretty as Alan had suggested. Ellie, the dark-haired one, attached herself to 'the new boy'. Greta was pleased to waltz with Alan. The thought did pass through his mind: 'how nice it would be, to have a girl of one's own'.

He had nobody dependent upon him now, he had a good salary and was already highly thought of in the mill. They could give a return party at Rawnpore; so ran his thoughts. A birthday kiss and a good-bye one, Davie felt weak at the knees!

'Nice girls, Alan.'

'Very, but we'll lose them when they go to the hills for three months, they will fall for those b..... Army-types. They all do. It's the uniform.'

There were a few meetings, Sunday lunch and a well-chaperoned ride down to the Ganges, where they watched women washing clothes then pounding them on stones. The garments soon dried sparkling white.

'They bathe three times a day, it seems to be part of their religion. When there is light rain, at the beginning or end of the monsoon, I've seen them bathing, but holding up umbrellas to keep the rain off their heads,' said Alan.

The Hindu women walked so gracefully, carrying heavy chattis on their heads.

'What a superb carriage they have,' said Ellie.—

Davie said little. The contrast of the life of the river, the dozens of people carrying on their everyday tasks, and the two British girls dressed in fine sprigged muslin and wearing large hats, tied with satin ribbon, was overwhelming. Yet, oddly, he thought, 'I wish they would not giggle.'

'Two different worlds,' he said to Alan.

Then suddenly, without reason, two figures appeared before his eyes—two poorly clad girls, one with long, black hair. She was picking primroses and the face which turned to him was Mary's. It was crazy that he should suddenly see her face so clearly. 'I wonder what has happened to her,' he thought.

However, these were only a few highlights in a usually boring routine—unbearable heat, grinding toil, endless patience in training native workers who spoke little English. Mostly, it would be easier to do the job oneself.

'Well, Davie you will soon have been here six months, how about us asking for leave at the same time, and we can go to the hills together for a month in the hot season?'

'I had made up my mind not to stay longer than the six months' trial period.'

'Don't be daft, boy, you're doing well, this is a natural depression from the heat and the dust—we shall try to go to the hills together and you will feel different. I felt the same after my first six months.'

Without Davie's knowledge, Alan went to the manager.

'Davie is under the weather, sir. He is eating nothing. He needs some air. Could the roster be arranged that we have our month's leave together?'

'If the foreman agrees to relieve the other two machinemen, then yes.'

Two weeks later, Davie was summoned to the manager's office. Mr. Logie had a habit of cutting the ground from beneath one's feet: 'I'm so pleased you are happy with us, Cameron, you have settled down very well, but I think we should arrange your month's leave. The first year the climate always seems the worst. Because it is your first spell, would you like to go with Turner?'

What could Davie say? Certainly not 'No thank you, I'm going home now', it had to be 'Thank you, sir, that would be very kind.'

Late that night:

'The manager suggested that we go to the hills together Alan, as you suggested, and I couldn't say no.'

'How could you go home without seeing the Himalayas? After the monsoon you will feel better.'

There was a beautiful hotel in Darjeeling owned jointly by the Jute Mill and the Paper Mill—one of the perks for the workers. Free food and accommodation was provided for one month.

That month in the foothills was an experience Davie would never forget. The beauty of the countryside, the tea plantations, the colourful saris of the Indian girls, and an insight into the way 'the other half lived'—Army officers on leave and ladies of high fashion. They did meet Ellie and Greta, but they were different.

'Heads turned by Army uniforms, I'll be bound,' volunteered Alan.

Davie had never felt so well off, financially. It was pleasant to have a bank balance.

All too soon, they returned to the plains, and that engulfing machine house.

So life went on, with different parties, changes in manpower, tittle-tattle about white men who had native girls.

'Their own wives should be out here with them,' said Alan, 'not just splashing the hard-earned money about, at home.'

So two more years went past. Both Alan and Davie had become foremen, as personnel finished contracts, and went home. Life was now a little easier, physically, but they had more responsibility. It was strange how their lives were to run on parallel lines for so many years.

They had each had four months leave—two in which to travel and two months at home—but not at the same time. They could not both be away so long at the same time.

Davie had, of course, kept in close touch with Meggie. Alan's home leave came first. He had said quite forlornly one evening: 'I'll enjoy the rest, Davie. I've nobody of my own to visit, so I thought I would go to Scotland to see whether you have exaggerated the beauties of Ruary and of Inveraray. I'll buy a bicycle and tour with a pack on my back.'

In his letters, Davie had told Meggie about Alan, and how kind and helpful he had been to him, especially when he first arrived in Rawn-pore; and he was delighted when she wrote back to say, that she and Peter would be happy if Alan cared to make their home his base, for the two months. Alan needed some persuading.

'I don't want to be a nuisance to anybody.'

'If you have nothing better to do, you can always help with the harvest. You will be no burden.'

Alan accepted gratefully, and departed with a length of silk for Meggie, and gifts for Peter and the two children she now had.

Alan came back, saying he had stayed at the farm for five weeks, and that he had bought a bicycle with pneumatic tyres and with a three-speed gear. It had been expensive, but wonderful for getting around, and he had given it to Peter, when he left, as a small token of his gratitude.

The following year, 1905, it was Davie's turn to visit Linaird. Peter's father had retired, so they now lived in the big farmhouse where there was plenty of room. His parents were installed in the cottage and looked after the large vegetable garden. Davie called to see Willie, who was married and lived on the outskirts of London. He only stayed two days. They were kind, but once he and Willie had gone through the repertoire of 'Do you remember,' there was nothing to say. He took the overnight train from London to Aberdeen, and a long wearisome journey it was; but, at Aberdeen station, there stood Meggie, Peter and a lovely two-year old boy.

'Meet Peter David Munro junior.'

There was a lovely baby daughter waiting at the cottage.

What a reunion! They had a wonderful two months together. Davie had brought gifts of real silk, gold bracelets and some interesting Benares work, as well as a long wooden train for young Peter. He helped with the harvest, carried food to the fields, fed the calves and the chickens and entertained his nephew by imitating the birds. Life was very good but not complete.

'Have you heard from Mary recently?'

'No. She said in her last letter that she was going to a post in London, but I have not yet received her address,' answered Meggie.

The weeks passed all too quickly. He broke his journey south to visit his father in Ruary. He had aged a lot, but was cleaner and more affable. His young brothers and sisters were strangers to him. He gave them gifts and some money, but there was no relationship there any more.

Neil had a good post with a firm of importers in Southampton, but he did not visit Ruary.

So, refreshed and with many promises to write to Meggie, he set sail again for Calcutta.

Alan welcomed him back to Rawnpore.

Then the wheel of fate spun very fast—indeed, Davie was left gasping.

PART II

I

What a relief! Davie had arrived at the dusty, Indian village station just on time and was astonished to find several bullock gharis and three carriages awaiting the overcrowded train from Calcutta. These were indeed an unusual sight at the tiny Rawnpore station. There was so little shade—just a small area with six stone pillars and woven bamboo roofing.

Davie had been five years in Rawnpore now, and Alan six. They understood each other well, had their differences of opinion and lengthy arguments, but these only cleared the air and all was well again. The friendship was too valuable to both. Davie had had to be peacemaker so often at home in the cottages, between parents, brothers and sisters. All his life one of his recurring phrases was, 'The quietest way is the best.' Alan, too, had learnt from his orphanage days, what it meant to have a reliable friend whom one could trust absolutely. It was not as though they quarrelled about anything important—just silly things—who forgot what in the Calcutta order, whether a ball was 'out' at tennis, which hill station would be honoured by their next visit. Last year they had decided to go to different stations, Alan wishing to follow Greta. Then, two weeks before they were due to leave, while Alan sat alone after dinner, one of the other foremen said, 'David where is your Jonathan?' Alan had to laugh.

'Shake, Davie! It's just the heat.'

It really was an unnatural life. They had had words the night before, over the disappearance of precious tinned meat from their private cupboards, halfway through the month.

'We probably forgot to order it!' said Davie.

These stupid thoughts passed through his mind as he stood on the platform. He was nervous, too. The manager, who should have met the train, was down with dysentery; the paper on his machine had broken three times in as many hours, and it meant a lot of waste to be recycled. He thought, 'That new machineman isn't so good, he could not have been checking the stuff which came into the chest, through the beaters.'

'Ugh, it's this heat, what a time of day for a train to arrive! It had been late leaving Calcutta.'

He mused on, 'He could not get to the hills soon enough.' Alan was right, too.

'Davie, it is only good sense to see as many of the hill stations as possible, we are not going to be here forever.'

'Heaven forbid, this is definitely my last year.'

He felt really off colour and hoped he was not going down with malaria again. Malaria was one of the curses of Rawnpore, which lay low and too near the Ganges and the marshes. The mosquitoes were fierce at times. The white-men did swallow the daily quota of quinine supplied by the company, but one's system became used to it in time. When Davie came out at first, he would find his stomach upset and his ears ringing, but the native doctor, employed by the firm, forbade any lessening of the dose. Nobody thought of salt tablets either, there was no talk of dehydration in those days, out in Rawnpore, but Davie did notice that at meal-times, especially in the hot season, he covered his food with salt and felt better—even if thirstier. What were they all doing out here in this climate anyway?'

'Where is that blasted train?' he wondered. 'I had time enough and to spare.'

The train did arrive one hour later.

Instead of feeling nervous, he should feel honoured to be representing the manager, by receiving the new managing director, his wife, three children, nurse, governess and ayah, as well as the new office secretary, brought out personally by the director.

He would have quailed at the thought of this task, had he not remembered Sarah's words to him, 'Walk tall, Davie, walk tall, keep your chin up, laddie, you are as good as they come.'

That, plus the fact that the manager's wife, Mrs. Logie, was accompanying him, to receive the ladies, made him pull himself together. After all, in four years he had become the head foreman.

Here came the train, now more than an hour late.

He pulled in his chin, straightened his tie and walked over to Mrs. Logie, who had been talking to one of the 'jute wives'.

Dozens of natives—Hindus, Muslims, even a few Sikhs—jumped from the steps, emerged from the windows or descended from the roof, to stretch cramped legs or to find whether such a small station boasted a water-carrier or a seller of sweetmeats, but all eyes gazed in wonder as the passengers descended wearily from the first-class coach to the platform, no less than three memsahibs in elegant muslin dresses, three children, (two girls and a boy), and two gentlemen—one middle-aged and one in his late twenties. Even the engine driver found this scene, in the heat of the afternoon interesting. He shouted to the station porter in Hindustani and must have received the appropriate answer, for he grinned broadly and asked how long these Angrezi-log would remain in such a hole as Rawnpore.

Saints alive, thought Davie, this arrival would go down in the history of Rawnpore.

'Mr. Stuart, sir? Mr. Logie presents his apologies, he is suffering from dysentery and cannot meet you. I'm Cameron, Mr. Stuart, the head foreman.'

Meantime, Mrs. Logie was greeting the ladies and Mrs. Stuart moved towards the end of the platform to check the luggage—helped by the secretary. There was an incredible amount of it—all the paraphernalia of the European in the Far East. It would take four bullock gharis to take that mountain of possessions.

Suddenly, a cold hand seemed to clutch at Davie's heart. It really could not be—it would be too cruel—but it was, it really was, Archibald McCulloch from his own village of Ruary.

'So, you have arrived in Rawnpore, Archie. Come this way, the porters will look after the luggage.'

For the life of him, he could not say 'Welcome' nor offer his hand.

'So, it's you Cameron. Don't bother, I'll accompany the young ladies. I travelled with them from London.'

'For this, have I given up my siesta,' he thought.

But he must think of his duty. There was laughter and stretching of legs; the children of seven, five and three, looked exhausted.

'Imagine bringing children of that age to this unhealthy place,' thought Davie. 'They cannot know that white children are buried all over the Indian plains because of the climate.'

Introductions were in progress and Davie was to have the second shock of the day. It is true that life can be stranger than fiction and here was proof. As he shook hands with the governess, he raised his eyes. The shock to both was electric. Davie was absolutely speechless, but his eyes spoke volumes. All Mary could say was, 'Davie!'

He turned in a daze to find Mr. Stuart at his elbow.

'I think we can get into the carriages now, Cameron.'

'Yes indeed, sir, the sooner the better.'

Archie was somewhat deflated to find that he had to live in the large Burra Bungalow with the other bachelors from the mill.

Davie was shattered that he had to live under the same roof as a McCulloch of Ruary.

Davie had never allowed himself to bear a grudge against anyone, but he was shocked to find that the old hurt and intense dislike of McCulloch, which he had long since almost forgotten, flooded back into his heart and mind, into his very soul. that period of his early childhood became as yesterday.

Davie helped Mrs. Logie and the Stuarts to alight from the carriage, then turned to go to Mary, but Archie was there first. Davie had had no opportunity to speak to Mary. He sat on the verandah of Shangri—the enormous bungalow in the middle of the compound, reserved for the director—and waited for Mrs. Logie, whom he must escort back to her own home.

Mary, Linda the Nanny, and the Ayah, had to busy themselves with the children who were fretful, so all Mary could do was to cast a longing glance and smile at Davie as she passed.

How beautiful she had become! So elegantly dressed! The raven hair and large, thoughtful grey eyes were just the same but she walked with an elegant assurance which became her well. Linda, too, made a good impression, but Davie was too busy with his thoughts to look at anyone else, from being almost physically sick at the sight of Archie, to light-headed elation when he saw Mary? Now, in one second of time, he really knew what love meant. What of Mary? Perhaps she was promised to someone else at home. Had she met the ideal husband during the long years since they had met? She had known of Archie's early behaviour in Ruary. She could not possibly be interested in him!

How Davie had been able to answer intelligently the questions Mr. Stuart had asked about the mill, he would never know. Perhaps a guardian angel had arrived along with the devil.

In his modesty, it had not struck Davie that Mary might have been a little impressed with him. For the handsome, blond, curly-haired young man in topee and immaculate whites bore no resemblance to the urchin of Ruary.

☆   ☆   ☆   ☆

It was five o'clock, Davie jumped from the vehicle and dashed into his quarters. No Alan, of course, he was still at the works. Davie poured himself two doubles from his Scotch and downed them. Slowly, the numbness seemed to clear from his brain. He poured himself a third large Scotch and, unaccustomed to so much 'hard stuff', he sat in a daze for what seemed hours. When his kindly bearer came in, he looked at his young master with horror, threw a mosquito net over him and went to sit on the top step of the verandah, rocking backwards and forwards in his concern. When the sweat-soaked Alan toiled up the steps, he said, 'Excuse, Turner Sahib, please. Cameron Sahib is very sick. Come quick.'

In a few strides, Alan stood over Davie, looked at the half-empty bottle and helped to lift him into bed. At four o'clock in the morning, Alan found Davie awake but staring stupidly at the ceiling.

'Up, Davie my boy—come on, a douche, then tennis,' and he pulled Davie out of bed, wondering what the devil had happened. It was a poor, half-hearted game. Several cups of tea later: 'Well, friend, what frightful gaffe did you perpetrate yesterday? Did you forget to meet the train or what?

Davie looked at him dully. 'The devil from Ruary has arrived and with him, Mary.'

'Come on now, pull the other one, I just don't believe you.' No reply.

'You really mean that Archie has arrived here in Rawnpore? I know the paper trade is a small world in itself, but really . . . '

'Yes, but he is not Archie any more,' and with an unaccustomed curl of his lip, 'he is Archibald. Mr. Archibald McCulloch, our new secretary.'

Alan had more sense than to ply his friend with questions.

'Well, thank God, he will be in the other bungalow—I heard today that there were rooms there for the new office-wallah, after all.

It was a body blow, Alan could see that, but left the subject for the moment. A hundred questions were trembling on his lips.

'Come on, Davie, or we shall be reporting late.'

Davie went through the motions of work—correcting the dye shade, advising the beaterman to add more soda ash. These past few months they had been using more woodpulp than esparto. There had been a fire in the esparto shed and they had to await the new shipment. A special boat had brought the woodpulp from upcountry, from the temperate zone. It was good to be so busy. Jimmy had been right to make him go to Lancashire for experience. Different chemicals were needed in the beaters. Alkaline liquors had to be added in correct quantity. Measures of size had to be altered to make the paper water resistant. Old machinery had to be cleaned, serviced and made workable. The engineers were bathed in sweat. Davie was anxious about his men—but he knew how salt helped him and he carried a small tin of it in his hip pocket as another might carry a flask, and now and then he made them take just a few grains. He was nicknamed 'the salt-cellar'—but the men were grateful for it. Davie had also made sure that there were vast quantities of boiled water standing on ice to compensate. He had to keep an eagle eye on the bales of pulp to make sure that there was not a mixture of hard wood bales, with soft wood pulp. No academy could have taught him all these points and more, it had been the long, hard grinding training which gave him the practical experience. The manager was still ill, no bouquets were presented to Davie and he expected no compliments. The knowledge that he could do it and take the responsibility gave him a quiet pride. 'Jimmy, you would be pleased with me.'

Only his men, black and white, knew what he had achieved for the mill.

To be so busy saved his reason. He had not seen Mary again and she had been in Rawnpore for three weeks.

After dinner one night, Alan ventured: 'You wished to speak to me, Davie?'

'You remember that we had decided this was to be our last year—that we had come here just to make a bit of cash and to hope for better jobs at home, after our experience? Now I have doubts. On the one hand, Rawnpore is too small to hold McCulloch and myself at one and the same time. On the other hand, I find that I really love Mary and I wish to be near her.'

'Well, we don't have to give notice for three months yet, and there will be our right to six weeks in the hills, so we shall do nothing in the meantime. Besides, I hear that the Nanny, Linda, is quite a girl.'

'They all travelled out together on the 'S.S. Otanora' first-class, and McCulloch has ingratiated himself into the director's good books,' said Davie.

'Well, even if McCulloch was the life and soul of the company, you have said that Mary would remember him from childhood. Even with a veneer of polish, he will give himself away, Davie.'

'I hope so. I can only see him as a dark and vicious bully, with calculating eyes, clenched fists and his father's horse-whip behind him.'

'You have lost time being so busy at the mill, Davie, you must contact Mary as soon as possible.'

'But how? I can't just walk up to Shangri.'

'No, but you can write a letter and send your bearer with it.'

The letter was sent and Mary replied that there was to be a reception soon at Shangri, so that Mr. Stuart could meet all the staff informally. She would see Davie then.

The Sunday of the reception arrived. Ram and Asi saw to it that their young masters were impeccably turned out and, indeed, they looked striking. At twenty-eight years, each sported a moustache—Alan's dark and clipped, Davie's curling blond on his lip.

'Well, here goes,' said Alan cheerfully. 'I'll be right behind you, if you meet your devil.'

To himself Davie whispered, 'Chin up and walk tall.'

'Ah, the young head-foreman who met us at the station and Mr. Alan Turner, my dear,' explained Mr. Stuart. 'Drinks here for the young sahibs, Akem!'

There in the middle of the much cared-for and well-watered lawn, under a shady tree, were Mary, Linda, the Ayah and the children.

Davie only had eyes for Mary. She was so beautiful—dressed in rose silk trimmed at neck and wrists with Maltese lace and carrying a matching parasol. She turned and looked at him and gave the old, slow, winsome smile.

'Davie, I fear I'm dreaming, that I'm suffering from the heat.'

He managed to utter, 'Mary,' and raised her fingers to his lips.

Discreetly, Alan moved over to Linda.

'They have forgotten to introduce us, I am Alan Turner, Davie's friend, and you must be Miss Linda.' He nodded to the Ayah and to the children, saying, 'Hello, welcome to Rawnpore.'

The two young bachelors could not monopolise the attention of two such attractive young ladies—but they did not move far off.

Mary appeared nervous. She had lived through much of the feud in Ruary between the cottagers and the McCullochs, and Aunt Sarah had kept her advised about the vendetta. If Archibald were to meet Davie now, sparks would certainly fly, and a row would be most unseemly at this reception.

'Mr. Turner, I know I have just met you, but Davie said you were his very good friend. Well . . . , er . . . , '

'Don't worry, Miss Mary, I know what is troubling you. I won't leave Davie in case he meets McCulloch.'

'I am most grateful. We are going to find ourselves in some very difficult situations. I have not told Mrs. Stuart about 'THE feud'—I merely said I had met Archibald in childhood. Now I must tell her about Davie, also.'

Alan and Davie strolled round the lawn. Monkeys were chattering in the trees, the bigger ones hurling mangoes at their mischievious offspring. A rustle near the hedge made them instantly alert. Poisonous snakes, including cobras, abounded in the area. There were many native servants on guard and the party was being highly successful—until they rounded the corner of a little summerhouse, offering shade, and came face to face with McCulloch, who was embracing one of the guests—a young niece of Mrs. Stuart, who had come up from Calcutta for a week or two. There was startled dismay on the faces of all four, then a sudden focussing of Archie's eyes on Davie. Poor Isobel fled, scarlet with embarrassment.

'The leopard does not change his spots.'

'You b..... well mind your own business, Cameron. Get out of my way and stay out until I have you sacked.'

'Glad to, McCulloch.'

With dignity, Davie moved away, followed closely by Alan. They withdrew to the far end of the lawn and watched, but Archie did not reappear.

'I always thought you might be exaggerating about his womanizing, Davie, but that one is a bastard, if ever I saw one.'

'Now, you see why we must warn the girls.'

'Indeed I do, we will make sure there is no trifling there.'

'Thank heaven, the rotter lives in the other bungalow. We must avoid crossing his path; for I swear I'll kill him, if he lays a finger on Mary.'

'Agreed. I'll do the same, should it be Linda. The ladies will be going to the hills in a month's time. We are due six weeks leave. We can follow them, when we find out where,' said Alan.

'And McCulloch will not have been here long enough to qualify for leave; but where that one wills, he has his way,' added Davie.

2

Mary was the eldest of ten children, among them triplets who died in infancy. Davie was the eldest of twelve, two of whom died in infancy. Perhaps this was the reason why later she and Davie had only one. The two strains seemed to have exhausted themselves, or was it a deep-seated psychological rejection of crowds of ill-fed children? Mary had been more fortunate than Davie. Her father was a highly skilled precision toolmaker, employed in one of the Clyde shipyards. For the times, his pay was supposed to be adequate—two pounds weekly, a little more with overtime. At least ten shillings remained in George's pocket. The precision toolmakers had, at one time, asked for more money. It was granted—the huge sum of one farthing per hour extra.

Two pounds in the city was different from two pounds in the country, where one could have a vegetable garden or keep chickens.

The Chisholms—George and Jane—lived in a tenement flat which had two bedrooms, a kitchen and an inside toilet, just for themselves. They were very fortunate. In some tenements, one toilet had to serve four or five families. The kitchen, as in most of the flats, boasted a box bed and both bedrooms, as well as double beds, had box beds.

George Chisholm was a true Victorian father. He worked long, hard hours and he demanded much. He was selfish and overstrict with the children, who feared him greatly. Looking back, Mary felt that she had never loved her father, although she was his favourite. After the third child arrived, George succumbed to the common habit of spending his evenings in public houses which had sawdust covered floors, brown paint, ill-kempt men and much argument.

He was six feet tall and what, in the bourgeoisie would have been beautiful hands with long slim fingers, but as a yard worker these long, tapering fingers suffered cuts and weals and had an everlasting smell of oil. Although he drank much more than he could afford, Mary had never seen him the worse for liquor.

Her mother, Jane, was a kind, gentle, country soul, brought up on a croft in Morayshire. Her parents died when she was seventeen and when her brother Frank returned from sea, he took the young Jane to friends in Glasgow, where she was apprenticed to a furrier. She met the fine, upstanding young George at a friend's house, and when she was twenty she married him and they made their home in Port-Glasgow. Had she had to spend her life in the big city she would have died. But in Port-Glasgow she could look from the tenement windows straight over the Clyde estuary, she could see all the river traffic and hear the gulls scream. Up to the time that she had four childsren, she had been able to pack bread and butter and carry bottles of milk or water in the pram, and take the children to Princes Pier or even to Gourock on the train to watch the great liners from all over the world, lying at the 'tail of the bank'. From the back of Princes Pier they could watch passengers embarking or disembarking. The arrivals were such happy occasions with the band playing welcoming tunes, but the departures were sad affairs with the band playing 'Will ye no come back again?'. The children loved the streamers which the wind often blew in their direction. Later, three of Jane's sons sailed away from Princes Pier to emigrate. In memory, it never seemed to be winter, never cold or wet and miserable. The sun always seemed to shine on sparkling waters, which mirrored the lovely hills behind. When they went to Gourock, they would stop at the fisherman's hut near the pier and buy thirteen herrings for five pence.

As the family increased rapidly, Jane could no longer take them on such outings but from the time that she was nine, Mary took the younger ones. When she was twelve, various neighbours entrusted their offspring to her safekeeping and once, on board the train, with children filling the carriage, the ticket collector asked, 'Have you not got any more under the seat?'

Every Saturday afternoon she could be seen trundling the old pram along with two infants in it and others trailing along behind.

Mary was very intelligent. At twelve, she won a free place in the grammar school. By this time, there were six children and another on the way. George was impatient.

'What good is schooling to a girl? She will be married in a few years.'

Jane wept bitter tears, but to no avail. Mary was up at half-past five every morning and did a milk round before school. On Saturdays, she helped in a baker's shop and proudly brought home her four shillings each week. It was good to help at the baker's. She could buy 'end' loaves at half price and often there were cakes and buns given away late on Saturday evening. With nine to feed, this was most welcome. From twelve to fourteen, Mary worked half-time and went to school for the other half.

Mary knew that her father spent too much money on drink; one dreadful week he only gave Jane one pound to feed nine people. So, although she was a naturally timid and highly-strung child, she decided something had to be done about it. Her father was paid at midday on Saturdays, so she arranged that her mother should have father's meal ready just after two o'clock. At twelve years of age, she would go into his favourite haunt about two o'clock, and take her father by the hand saying 'Father, your dinner is getting cold, come for it now.' Secretly pleased that his daughter cared so much, George would frequently get up like a lamb, take her little hand and go home. At other times, as an act of bravado, he would hand her most of the two pounds and sit on with his cronies. Occasionally, some other foolish father would hand her a few coppers for herself. Mary, therefore, learnt very early in life, to save coppers and to waste nothing.

On her way home from school one day, she caught sight of a notice in the window of a very elegant dressmaking-establishment.

'Wanted, a polite, refined girl to learn dressmaking. Apply within.'

So, Mary entered the establishment to ask if she might be engaged. The wages would be three shillings weekly for the first year and, after twelve hours in the shop, she would often have to deliver gowns to clients. The child hopped and skipped all the way home, she was so delighted, but she meant to wait until the younger children were in bed before she broached the subject.

Alas, good fortune was not with her. Father came in and without preamble said, 'I've found a good job for Mary. Tailor, the butcher, wants a girl to scrub counters and clear out the back shop.' Mary felt sick. Consternation was written all over Jane's face.

'What's the matter then?'

'That work is much too hard for Mary. She is small and slim and not fit for such heavy work. She deserves something better, the way she has been earning for years.'

'Nonsense, Jane, she will start tomorrow morning. I have said so.'

'George Chisholm, in all the years we have been married, I have never disobeyed you, until now. Mary will NOT start in the butcher's scrubbing counters and cleaning out a dirty, smelly back shop. I forbid it.'

He lifted his great hand to strike her, but she was a little thing and heavily pregnant and his hand stopped in mid-air.

'We will sleep on it until tomorrow.'

There was always dead silence when father spoke. The children cowered into corners.

Mary knew she was his favourite, so she bided her time. After he had eaten, calmed down and stretched full length in the easy chair half-asleep: 'Father,'—there were no diminutives in that house—'if we were well off, do you know what I would like to do?'

The others were in bed, including Jane who felt weak after the row.

'We are not rich, so spare me the nonsense.'

'Well, I like to imagine, Father. If I could sew as well as Mother, I could make clothes for all of us . . . and'—with a rush before he could get a word in—'Mrs. Laird at the gown shop has a notice in the window, she wants a learner. Three shillings a week.'

No reply.

68

'If I continued my milk round and worked at the baker's on Saturday afternoon—that would be six shillings and sixpence per week. I'll
make you a fine cap in no time, Father.'

George pretended to be asleep. This elfin child with jet black hair
waving to her waist, the little fringe, the big grey eyes and the pale
complexion—he remembered that they nearly lost her twice—the first
time at a month old, and not so long ago, when she had scarlet fever.

'Well, you can try it for a month. Frank will have to bring my tea to
the yard when I work overtime. He is eleven now.'

In high glee, she told her mother next morning.

'I have already got the job. Mrs. Laird said so yesterday.'

'Mary, you are the only one who can get round him. We must not
cross him tonight.'

'So Mary learnt to make skirts—but not jackets. Mrs. Laird was wily
enough to know that, if her girls could make coats as well as skirts, they
could start up in opposition.

After a year, Mary asked to see the lady in question.

'Mrs. Laird, could I learn now to make coats, please?'

'Certainly not, Mary—not for years yet.'

Mary shot a long bow, 'I'm very sorry, madam, I shall have to leave
then. I must learn to make coats.'

'You can leave then, young miss. You will be in trouble—go now.'

'Thank you, Mrs. Laird I shall be all right. Mrs. Harris'—the other
elegant dressmaker in town—'needs a girl in coats.'

Mary could scarcely open the door to leave, her knees were knocking.

'Mrs. Harris, indeed, how dare you move there. You can go to coats
but you will remain on three shillings weekly for another year.'

Mary floated as on a cloud.

Jane said, 'Now, Mary, on no account must you tell your father, he
will thrash you. We will find the extra sixpence you should now be
earning, somehow or other.' 'Frank, take those empty jam jars back to
the grocer. I need the threepence.'

At Christmas, Mary received a letter from her good friend Meggie
Cameron, whom she had met when she was staying with Aunt Sarah.
This was a great thrill. She had liked Meggie and her brothers very
much, especially the Davie one. They had included her in all their fun,
paddling, picnicking and trying to catch trout with their hands. That
had been a wonderful holiday. It had almost been worth having scarlet
fever and going to hospital for that reward. She loved Ruary and would

love to go back to Aunt Sarah's—but there was no money and no opportunity.

The rest of the news interested her too. Meggie was a 'Tweenie' in a big house in Aberdeenshire and was very happy. Davie was actually living at Rose Cottage with Aunt Sarah. Somehow she must go back to Ruary one day.

'Read my letter, Mother, it is from Meggie Cameron. I must reply before New Year.'

At seventeen, Mary was an excellent needlewoman. She could cut out the most intricate patterns and, secretly, Mrs. Laird found her help invaluable. Her manners were pleasing and she spoke well. She was entrusted to deliver the most expensive gowns, coats and cloaks to the wealthy ladies of the town. Sometimes, the lady would tip her twopence. This was never wasted. Mrs. Laird also permitted her to take home end pieces of material, or lace—all of which was received gratefully.

When Mary had first entered Mrs. Laird's gown shop, she found, to her astonishment, that one of the dressmakers was a Frenchwoman, who spoke very poor English. She had married a Scot, but was now a widow. In no time, in order to while away hours of boring work, undoing a hem, shortening or lengthening garments, she would repeat words after Louise. After three years, she could carry on a simple conversation in French.

'Que tu parles bien alors, ma petite!'

Despite the little free time she had, Mary discovered the Public Library. After fifteen, she was allowed to take books home. She read avidly after the chores were done. She loved the glossy magazines at Mrs. Laird's and read those, if there were a few minutes to wait for a garment. Mary was living on her nerves and doing far too much. One day, she fainted at work, she could not eat, if she did she was always sick. Jane had to send for the doctor. Instead of treating her for nervous exhaustion, the stupid man decided she had been poisoned and pumped out any contents left in her stomach. That finished Mary with doctors for many a year to come.

Frank shouted, 'The two Aunts are at the door, Mother, asking for you,' and when Jane went, there stood Flora and Dora, George's two sisters, who lived in Glasgow.

'We have not seen you for years, so we have come with the fine weather.'

'How many children have you now, Jane?'

'Seven, Flora, the triplets died.'

'Maybe as well. You have nowhere to sleep them.'

'It is time you stopped,' said Dora.

'I'd be glad if you would tell that to George.'

'Where is Mary?'

'Poor Mary is ill in bed, she has had a terrible doing. The doctor pumped out her stomach this morning and she is in a state.'

Flora marched into the bedroom, took one look at the quivering child and said: 'You will just come back to Glasgow with Dora and me, until you have had a rest, for you won't get it here.'

'I can't, Auntie Flora, Mother needs my money.'

'You will just come. We can spare a few shillings to leave with your mother. Let us have some tea, Jane, then we will be going.'

Meantime, Dora started to empty a black bag. Out came home-made scones and sponge cake—the like of which Mary had not tasted for years. At Flora's command, Mary ate a morsel of sponge and took a few sips of tea.

'I told you it would stay down. We'll have no more nonsense.'

Tears of weakness were the only answer.

'I don't know what George will say.'

'You leave George to me, Jane. I'll soon sort him out.'

So, Mary went to Glasgow for two weeks and had the rest and change she needed. They walked sedately in Kelvingrove Park and round the University. They went to the Bromielaw to watch the different steamers arriving and departing amid much excitement.

'We watch them from the window in Port Glasgow, but it is fun to see so many here.'

Then, later, 'Aunties Flora-Dora, Mother needs a holiday. If I stay only one week, could she come for the second week and I would look after the family?'

'Certainly not, you will stay two weeks. We shall see to your mother later. She will have to do without you, one day, won't she?' said Flora.

Towards the middle of the second week, when Mary was much stronger, Flora and Dora nodded to each other and said: 'We'll go tomorrow.'

Mary had not laughed so much for years. It was a tonic just to be with the Aunts, they were so different from their brother. Whatever one said, the other agreed with, so that Mary just called them Auntie Flora-Dora and it pleased them.

'What are you plotting for tomorrow?'

Dora looked mischievous but would say nothing. Flora and Dora had never married, but they were not sour old spinsters. Flora was cheerful and extrovert, Dora was quiet and thoughtful, so that they complemented each other.

To earn a living, they rented a small shop in a busy street, in a good area. From the end of the street they could see Kelvingrove Park and the University. They sold tobacco and cigarettes, sweets, lemonade and, often, home-made cakes. It was a very busy life and they worked from half-past-seven in the morning until there was no longer any evening trade. Fortunately, they lived at the back of the shop—very cosily and on the spot. They lived frugally, too, for they knew that they would have to keep themselves in their old age. They never imagined in 1900 that there would be a modest old age pension for them in later life.

Very occasionally, as a treat, they would shut the shop and take a day off. There was an old tea-caddy on the kitchen shelf, which they used as a savings-box for outings. They put all their farthings into it, then changed these into pennies, into shillings—right up to crowns. Then they would spend hours and hours deciding where to go. The tin had several crowns in it, it was a lovely warm spell in June and Mary was here, so, 'Where shall we go, Flora?'

'To Arrochar, of course, Dora.'

They were so thrilled that there was money enough for three.

It was one of the most beautiful days imaginable. One magnificent scene followed another, all day long. Dora was a reader and knew much of the local history.

'Look at Dumbarton Rock. It is called the Gibraltar of Scotland. This was one of the chief ports when Scotland had its own navy.' And later, she added, 'Mary of Scotland sailed from here to become Queen of France.'

'Don't talk so much, Dora, let Mary look at the scenery.'

'It is very hot,' said Dora.

'Well, I told you not to wear four petticoats today, and your white blouse will soon be covered with smuts from the engine.'

'You both look very nice in your shady bonnets,' said Mary, who had had much practice in being a peacemaker.

At Craigendoran, they changed from the North British Line to the West Highland. Mary looked across the Firth and wondered how the family were faring. She felt guilty enjoying herself so much.

All three were ecstatic. Weren't the seats comfortable?—like armchairs on the West Highland line to Loch Lomond and, to Tarbert. Tarbert and Arrochar were served by the tiny station.

They walked down to the magnificent Tarbert Hotel. It looked like a castle. After a meal, they climbed into an open horse-drawn brake. These brakes plied between Tarbert and Arrochar. Many visitors came to Tarbert by steamer from Bowling, so the owners of the brakes were kept busy.

Only about two miles separated the two hamlets, but they were wonderful miles separating Loch Lomond from Loch Long.

'Mary, long ago the Vikings sailed to Arrochar and carried their longboats and oars across this neck of land to Loch Lomond where they carried on pillaging.'

'Let us have our picnic down at the shore,' interposed the practical Flora. 'There will be a cool breeze from the hills of Argyll.'

Their bottles of cold tea were very welcome.

Mary vowed that one day she would go all the way to Fort William on the train, and she did.

Too soon, good-byes had to be said, and Mary returned to Port Glasgow a totally different young lady.

3

When Mary was twenty-two, she received a long letter from Meggie, giving her lots of news. 'Imagine, Mary, I was married last week to a wonderful young farmer called Peter Munro. We live near Ellon in Aberdeenshire.' She went on to extol the virtues of Peter and was obviously very much in love.

'Davie came all the way from England to give me away. It was very good of him, because he is leaving soon for India—but you know Davie. You DO remember him, don't you? The main point of my letter is a message for you. Yes, Davie asked whether I heard from you and where you were. No, Mary, that is not the main point. It is as follows.'

'My former mistress, Mrs. Anderson, came to my wedding and asked me whether I knew of a young lady, pleasant, honest, reliable, who would go to her sister in England as governess. Don't shake your head, Mary—it is only to teach reading, writing and the rudiments of arithmetic, and to be responsible for three children, aged seven, five and three, in a general way. Mrs. Anderson's sister, called Mrs. Stuart, does not keep very well. There is a nanny there also, and a cook-housekeeper, so your work would be quite pleasant. I met this Mrs. Stuart, also Sir Geoffrey's sister, once, when I went back to Ruary with Mrs. Anderson. She seemed quite nice.'

'If you are interested, Mrs. Anderson said you could suggest going on three months' trial. They are rich and all your expenses would be paid. The Stuarts have a house on the Thames not far from Maidenhead. Now that your brothers and sisters are growing up, it would be a nice change for you. Do write to Mrs. Stuart, here is the address. Love from Meggie.'

So, Mary went South to a beautiful home standing in acres of ground, to a pleasant family. Mrs. Stuart had replied to her letter, saying that she thought the three months' trial was a good idea. Could she possibly come within a month? Enclosed was money for her fare and expenses.

Mary liked the children, saw little of the father, found the mother rather querulous, spending much of her day on her chaise-longue, but the poor soul seemed rather delicate. Mary found that she really was *in loco parentis*. She had complete charge of the children—she had had experience enough of that—bought their clothes, arranged their outings, instructed them. Because Nanny did all the practical jobs, Mary found her work far from onerous. She wrote home: 'To think I earn forty pounds per year, receive an allowance for clothes, because I accompany the family when the children are with them, and all my keep. I shall be able to send you money from time to time.'

After the three months, Mr. Stuart said, 'We are very happy that you are here, Mary. Will you stay on with us? Mrs. Stuart and I would be grateful if you would continue to teach the children as much as you can, until they are old enough to go away to school. Please use the library as much as you want.'

About a year later, when they were at table, the surprise came.

'I have been asked to go to India for a year, Mary. Mrs. Stuart and the children will, of course, accompany me. We should be delighted and grateful if you would come with us to take full charge of the children. We shall ask Nanny to come, also.'

'May I think the matter over? I still feel a responsibility for my mother and the younger children.'

'We can arrange that, by having my London Secretary mail money each month to your mother. We would, of course, offer you ten pounds more per annum.'

'Then, thank you, Mr. Stuart, I shall be delighted to accompany the family.'

They were to sail in three months.

Mrs. Stuart said, 'You must realise, Mary, that we are going to a very hot and humid part of India. You will find the heat overpowering, but we shall, of course, go to the Himalayas during the hot season.'

Mr. Stuart added, 'We shall go to Scotland for the summer, as usual, and sail from Southampton in September. We shall stay with Sir Geoffrey at Ruary. You and Nanny can have six weeks to visit your family and acquire suitable clothing. I will give you a list of requirements. Then we shall all meet in Maidenhead early in September.'

'Are you sure you want to go so far away, Mary?' asked her mother.

'It is only for a year, I like the children and it is a wonderful opportunity to travel.'

'Travelling with three children and a sick mistress won't find you a husband,' said Father.

'I will perhaps find the husband when I return, and I will still send Mother the same amount of money until I return.'

'Mary, you say that Mrs. Stuart has given you a good dress allowance. Well, we can make your underclothing and simple dresses, but go to Mrs. Laird and order your gowns and cloaks—to be ready in two weeks!' Jane added, 'And watch her face!' Mary's laughter was a joy to hear.

Mrs. Laird was astounded, speechless and confused, when Mary walked in and ordered travelling clothes, thick and thin, and several silk and muslin gowns.

Louise—Mary's former French colleague chuckled happily—because, when Mary had left to go south, Mrs. Laird had predicted all sorts of calamities, repeating, 'You will be glad to come back, very glad.' Because she made so many garments herself, she was able to give her mother a new outfit and boots for all the children. Things were not so difficult now. Most of the family were earning. Now, the home looked neater, also. Jane had always kept herself neat and tidy, despite the demands of so many children. George, too, had improved. He was drinking less—probably because some of the pressure of too big a family had been removed. After a ship had been fitted out, the men were allowed to buy pieces of mahogany and small pieces of brass. With his long, tapering fingers he had started to fashion pokers with interesting handles, fire-dogs, sewing boxes. And pay they did for the wood and metal. The fear of gaol kept the weaker ones honest.

Mary grieved that Sarah and Jimmy were no longer in Ruary. She had loved them and would never forget the weeks she spent with them. She did go to Glasgow to say good-bye to Flora-Dora, and they were delighted at the opportunity coming her way. Mary had even written to Meggie and they arranged to meet for a day at Perth. They had a very happy time. Meggie was upset because she had forgotten to bring the slip of paper with Davie's address on it.

'I promise to send it to you, Mary, when you let me know where to write.'

'India is an enormous country, Meggie, we probably would not be within a thousand miles of each other.'

'Promise to visit us next year, when you return.'

Even George arrived home on time and stayed to chat, on Mary's last evening.

'We shall miss you, lass, you have been a great help to us.'

There was dead silence. The whole family were astounded that George should admit so much. To think that Father had actually praised someone. When Jane had recovered, she made her little speech: 'Now, Mary, you must write to us regularly. I'm not happy at your travelling to the ends of the Earth, but you are now nearly twenty-two and all the woman you will ever be. You know right from wrong and that is all I have to say.'

'Goodness, of course I shall write. Anyway, I'm not away for life—only for a year. It will pass in no time.'

So, Mary set out for the South and, ultimately, India. Fortunately, it was a school day for the youngest members of the family, and the others were at work. She could not have borne to have the whole family at the station. The previous day, Mary had ordered a cab—one of the old 'grumblers'—to pick her up. Jane and Ellen, the neighbour whose children Mary had taken on so many picnics, accompanied her to the station. All she carried was a gladstone bag and a roomy handbag. Her large cabin trunk marked 'Wanted on voyage' had been taken to the station the previous evening, by the 'stickman'. It had been too big for any cab. Frank and the stickman had roped it on to his small handcart and Frank had accompanied him to help with the lifting. She hoped that it was still safely in the stationmaster's office.

As she gazed at her daughter in the station, after the trunk had been safely deposited in the guard's van, Jane thought how beautiful she had become and that she certainly had acquired a dress sense. That dove-grey outfit was an ideal travelling costume.

The through carriages to King's Cross were very clean and comfortable, but it was a long, slow and tedious journey and so unwise to open a window for air, or one was sure to get a smut in the eye or on one's clothes.

'Oh, Mr. Stuart, how kind of you to meet me yourself. Linda—so you DID arrive first.'

The house near Maidenhead had been closed and caretakers installed, so they all proceeded to a large flat in Paddington.

'Thank goodness you are here,' said Russell, with all the importance of a seven-year-old. 'Mother said you might take wrong connections, but I knew you would not, Miss Mary.'

'Thank you for your confidence in me, Russell. How are Elisabeth and Margaret?'

'They are over-excited, Mother says, so we are not to talk too much about the journey.'

Elisabeth greeted Mary shyly, Margaret looked peaky.

Mr. Stuart said, 'We shall be here for five days—I must check all our documents and luggage.'

'What a mountain of luggage,' laughed Linda, the Nanny. 'It completely fills this big bedroom, and it is all labelled differently.'

'Someone has been very busy,' said Mary.

'Not required on voyage,' 'Needed on voyage,' 'For cabin use,' 'Fragile—with care,' 'This side up.'

Mrs. Stuart asked, 'Have you both packed two trunks, one for cabin use, the other to go into the hold?'

'No,' exclaimed Mary, 'I did not think of that.'

Linda also shook her head.

'Don't worry, there is still time. Go out tomorrow and buy two TIN trunks for the hold. You still have time to re-pack.'

'So, that adds four more trunks to ours,' shouted Russell cheerfully.

'Linda, it looks as though we are off for years and years.'

'Not I,' said Linda. 'One year will be enough for me.'

With the help of the gardeners and handyman from Maidenhead, the mountain of luggage eventually arrived at Paddington.

'So, tomorrow we are off,' said Mrs. Stuart.

'Father has booked a whole compartment on the Southampton train,' volunteered Elisabeth.

'Good gracious why?' asked Mary. 'The big luggage will all be in the guard's van.'

Russell knew all about it. 'Well we are seven, and several friends, aunts and uncles are coming to wave us good-bye. Then there is all our personal hand luggage.'

'Linda, have you got all the children's necessities, face cloths, towels, eau-de-cologne, medicines and toys for the voyage?'

'I hope so,' breathed Linda fervently.

It was a different world—a complete revelation to Mary and Linda. It was good that they had each other, and even better that they were good friends. They travelled first-class and had a suite of cabins, all with portholes. Happily, there were communicating doors between cabins for Mary, Linda and the children.

The farewells were incredible. They surpassed anything that the child Mary had witnessed at Princes Pier. The scene brought a lump to her throat and she thought of a group of poor children, picnicking on bread and jam and bottles of liquorice water, whom she had shepherded on many an occasion to the grass near Princes Pier.

She did appear to be on the crest of a huge wave. Life was wonderful.

The farewells had, indeed, been incredible. Masses of flowers everywhere, letters and telegrams, shouts of 'bon voyage', bands and the inevitable streamers, breaking as they drew away from the dock. And so to tea.

4

The shock came at dinner that evening. As they proceeded to the dining room—Mary and Linda were to remain alternate evenings with the children—and took their places a dark-haired young man, rather heavily built and with an ingratiating smile, joined them.

'Ah yes, my dear, this is our new Rawnpore secretary—Mr. Archibald McCulloch. Miss Chisholm this is Mr. McCulloch.'

She could not be mistaken, but it was an extraordinary coincidence—the name McCulloch—a young man, heavily jowled, suave, rather too attentive. Her memory switched back to that lovely summer in Ruary, to Meggie to the tales she had heard of the McCullochs. She decided to say nothing, but his arrival had spoilt her appetite. She simply bowed but did not take the proffered hand. Fortunately, the steward was at her side, so the action was not noticeable.

'It must be the same creature,' she thought miserably, the joy of a moment ago fading away. 'I will say nothing, not even to Linda, unless he gets too familiar.' From Calcutta, she must write to Meggie for Davie's address. He must be told that Archie was in India. The paper trade is a world of its own. He and Archie would be bound to meet, thought Mary.

'I'm glad we are out of the Bay of Biscay, now,' moaned poor Mrs. Stuart. She and Elisabeth had had a very bad time. It had been very stormy. To Russell's delight, the fiddles—nautical term to stop things from sliding off the table in bad weather—had had to be fixed on the tables. 'The stewards are amazed that I am here for all the meals,' he crowed.

There were long, halcyon, sparkling days through the Mediterranean, a misery of heat in the Red Sea, then, at last, they entered the Indian Ocean.

Ship's officers were only too delighted to chat about flying fish, peculiar currents and changes in the water colour to two attractive young ladies.

Unfortunately, previous acquaintance with Archie had to be divulged. When Mrs. Stuart was on her feet again, she had asked one evening, 'Which part of Scotland do you come from, Mr. McCulloch?'

'A tiny village, of which I am sure you have not heard, Mrs. Stuart.'

'Just where?'

'A tiny hamlet on the River Ripple in central Scotland.'

'RUARY, how extraordinary. We spend our summer holiday there each year. It is strange that we never met.'

'That is indeed incredible, Mrs. Stuart—probably I was away in college while you were there.'

Mary thought, 'That is a downright untruth. I wonder why he didn't wish the Stuarts to be aware of his connection with Ruary. After all, his father was an employee of Mrs. Stuart's brother.'

'And Miss Chisholm also has a link with Ruary.'

'Indeed?' He turned to Mary and looked rather foxy. 'I wonder why we never met? I would never forget such a beautiful young lady.'

Mary did not enlighten him, merely, saying, 'What a coincidence. Life is very strange, is it not?'

A few days later, Archie waylaid her on the promenade deck.

'Mrs. Stuart informs me that you are the niece of the late Mrs. Geddes of Rose Cottage in Ruary.'

'That is correct, Mr. McCulloch.'

'I knew Jimmy Geddes well. It is strange that we never met, when you came on holiday.'

'I only spent one holiday there, after an illness. It is a beautiful place. The old bridge and the river are so picturesque.'

'I feel I have seen you there.'

'Oh, I doubt it, I was very young at the time.'

From that time on, Archie paid Mary even more attention. He was attracted, of course, by her dignity and beauty, but some elusive memory kept teasing him. It was obvious to Mary that he meant to trap her, to find out the truth, and, of course, truth will out.

Within Archie's hearing one day, Linda asked Mary in all innocence, 'Did you remember to send Meggie a card before we left Aden? You said to remind you.'

'Yes, thank you Linda, I did remember.'

The word 'Meggie' was, of course, the key to the puzzle and Archie pounced.

'Did you mean Meggie Cameron?'

'Yes, I did.'

At once, he became sly and foxy.

'Now, I can place you—you were the girl who ran around with those dirty brats from the cottages. Where is that Davie creature now?'

The respect which he had paid her until now, disappeared in a flash. He had pinned her like a butterfly in a collection.

'You are speaking of my best friends, Mr. McCulloch, and I don't care to discuss them with you.'

'I'll see that you do, my beauty. I certainly have a bone to pick with you. So don't come Miss High and Mighty with me.'

Mary walked away, really shaken.

'Oh, Mary, did I say something wrong?'

'No, dear, I'll tell you some other time, but be very careful, that man is an out and out rotter.'

Mary had to be in Archie's company at times, but she took care never to be alone and she avoided sitting next to him at table, but she was very conscious that he was merely biding his time.

They called at Bombay, then sailed for the last lap round India. Shipboard life was as gay or as quiet as one cared to make it.

Mrs. Stuart insisted that the two girls went to at least some of the parties and the dances, but there were many unattached young men aboard—many of them soldiers returning to their regiments after home leave, so they managed to avoid a confrontation with Archie.

One evening, he caught her by the arm, hissing, 'Dance this one with me or I shall tell Mr. Stuart what I think of you and your youthful companions.'

His whisky-laden breath was much too close to her face for comfort and she began to be anxious, but a friendly young army captain, said, 'You did promise me this dance, I believe, Miss Chisholm.' She could have hugged him.

On this uneasy note, the ship docked in Calcutta and Archibald McCulloch made himself indispensable to the Stuarts. They thought he was wonderful. Even Linda, despite Mary's warning, was drawn to him.

'I can't understand why you are so cool and standoffish to Archibald. He is kind and has been so helpful with the children and the luggage.'

Mary was really unhappy. She would like to have confided everything that she knew about Archie, to Linda, but she could not do this without seeming prejudiced or even stupid. How could anyone understand her anger and aversion to an individual whom she had not met since she was ten years old? It was something to do with this curly-headed Davie, whom she also had not seen for the same long years. To her, this same Archibald was officious, overhelpful, intrusive, even offensive—at least, in his attitude to her.

On learning that the Stuarts were to spend a week in Calcutta, Archibald decided to do the same. Mr. Stuart was quite pleased, because he had so much business to discuss, importers and exporters to interview, the latest price sheets for woodpulp and esparto grass to peruse, shipping agents to consult, that McCulloch would be there to escort the ladies and the children.

McCulloch also, as the new secretary, would have to meet many of the business people concerned.

Despite the mountain of luggage she had brought with her, Mrs. Stuart wished to buy rolls of silk, tussore and muslin, as well as lace and ribbons suitable for all of them. It was better to see the articles, check and compare the prices, than write back from Rawnpore. Also, Mrs. Logie had been kind enough to recommend an ayah, whom she knew to be trustworthy and dependable, to help Nanny. So, ayah had to be interviewed also.

Lastly, warehouses and food stores had to be visited to buy suitable chairs for children, a small bed for Margaret and a store of mosquito nets. Their monthly order for extra food and delicacies had to be arranged—and sent upline to Rawnpore.

'Money is no problem,' said Linda.

'Happily, we shall share the goodies also.'

The great mass of luggage, greatly increased by the purchases in Calcutta, was put into the two railway vans and they proceeded en masse, with Ayah in attendance also, to the booked compartment of the slow, overcrowded train to Rawnpore.

Mrs. Stuart wailed, 'It is only supposed to be one hundred and fifty miles, but with all these natives clinging to the train, we shall never get there.'

At each major stop, provision had been made for them to receive cardboard boxes of suitable food, handed into the compartment. They had brought their own cases of beer and lemonade from Calcutta.

Finally, on a hot and dusty mid-afternoon, the slow train jerked to a halt at the little station of Rawnpore.

5

Gradually, the Stuarts and entourage settled into the huge bungalow 'Shangri'. Despite living in comparative luxury, it took them some time to settle into the new routine.

With Mrs. Logie, the ladies were the only memsahibs of the little village, and the arrival of two pretty young ladies caused much interest in the Burra Bungalow, especially after the reception on the lawn at Shangri.

There were also two Eurasian ladies in the community, but most of the men were bachelors or had wives at home who refused to live on the plains in India. It was really rather sad, thought Mary, that men toiled, sweated and grew old before their time, to keep wives and children in luxury, thousands of miles away.

How beautiful most of the native girls were—so graceful, charming and undemanding. They came from surrounding villages. A few would meet the white men sometimes at the post-dâk, they brought colour and comfort into a few drab, aimless lives. These, of course, were the men who stayed too long in the plains, who lost touch with the wives and families they supported so far away, and saw only once every two years. One or two had even retired early and 'gone native'. Most of the young bachelors had a different outlook, they were there to labour for a few years, to make some cash, which they could not earn in the homeland, or even just to gain experience: mostly both.

Few of them realised what conditions were really like, until they arrived on the plains.

Mr. Stuart had come out only for a short spell, because he was a large shareholder in the mill and he had heard conflicting stories about life and conditions in Rawnpore, and wished to see for himself. Like many businessmen of that era—after the long reign of the Empress Victoria and the accession of Edward VII—he wished to see where his money was invested and who was in charge of it.

As well as the white men, the mill provided work for whole Hindu families, and when new men arrived from abroad, somebody's bearer had a brother or a cousin, or a second or third cousin, who would like to serve the new sahib. On the whole, these servants were well-treated, some indeed became friends for life. If the manager heard of any cases of meanness, unkindness or injustice, the white boss was strongly reprimanded. It was, therefore, a close-knit community of black and white, mud huts and bungalows, and relations had to be kept good. It was fifty-four years after the Mutiny. It was to everyone's interest to live and let live in such a small, isolated community on the edge of the jungle. 'How would Archie fit in to such a community?' wondered Mary.

The children, too, settled down quite happily, after they got into their new routine. They got up at half-past-five in the morning, played with bats and balls or at croquet. After breakfast, they had lessons from half-past-seven until half-past-nine, then usually went for a ride, either to the river or to the bazaar. They were always accompanied by Ayah and either Mary or Linda, plus coachman and another servant carrying the usual pronged stick in case of snakes. Then there was tiffin, a long siesta and, after four o'clock, they played on the lawn or on the verandah.

There were punkahs in most rooms and lots of boys to pull the cords. Russell was much amused because two of them preferred to tie the cord around their big toes, lie on their backs, and pull, even if they dozed off themselves.

Eurasian and native children frequently came to play with the young Stuarts, so that, the climate apart, life was quite interesting for them.

The monkeys chattering in the trees they loved best of all. They threw mangoes at the children and the children threw them back again.

Mary had warned, 'It is better not to throw the mangoes back, in case you hit the monkeys. These are Hanumans and are worshipped by some of the castes, just as those cows, which we saw wandering around the bazaar, are.

The brightly coloured birds also fascinated them, 'Stay in the shade, now, and draw and colour as many birds as you can, then we shall find out their names.'

Russell's favourites were the elephants and their mahouts working at the Ganges—carrying enormous logs, or the elephants near the works, for they could lift great bales of grass or pulp with no apparent effort.

Only little Margaret did not appear to be happy. She remained just as languid as she had been in Maidenhead. During the sea-voyage, she had seemed much better. She was a sweet child and never complained but, at three years of age, she was content to sit on their laps and watch.

'Nanny and I both think you should ask the doctor to examine Margaret, Mrs. Stuart. Her pallor frightens us at times and she eats so little—only fruit.'

Dr. Sim, a Hindu, was a gentle, polite man, who had trained in London. He lived with his charming wife and two children in a large bungalow on the outskirts of the compound. He had been appointed by the firm to look after the health of all the mill employees, black and white. His two children had been sent to England to finish their studies and he was very proud that his elder son was studying medicine at Charing Cross Hospital. The Stuarts found the Sims very pleasant company.

'The climate here just does not suit Margaret, Mrs. Stuart. You must take her early to the hills. I detect a slight heart condition, also, so do not force her to run about. She must eat a little more, try her with sago into which whipped white of eggs has been added, then cool it on ice.'

The cookhouse was separate from the house and Ayah herself went to see that the dish was made attractive.

The young men from the Burra Bungalow were invited, in turn, to afternoon tea at Shangri. Naturally, the Stuarts preferred some to others and, fortunately, Davie and Alan were among those favoured. Because he had a good office appointment, and probably also because they had come to know him—or so they thought—on the voyage out, Archie was sometimes asked to dinner.

Davie and Alan also met the girls at the little mission chapel on Sundays.

'Do you go to church, Alan?'

84

'I used to, at the orphanage, but have long been careless about it.'

'I went to Sunday School with Meggie while I still had decent clothes.'

'Well we had better go, it will please the missionary, Mr. Beale. He has little support.'

'Come off it, Alan, we want to see the girls and we have little enough opportunity.'

'I am seriously interested in Linda and I know that you are in Mary, so could we not ask permission to call on them on Saturday and Sunday afternoons?'

'There would be no harm in asking Mr. Stuart's permission. He can only say no.'

'Yes, and we have a black cloud on the horizon, you know whom.'

Indeed, Archibald stood in such high favour with the Stuarts that remarks were made between husband and wife to the effect:

'Archibald is a regular caller. I am not sure which of the girls he favours,' said Mrs. Stuart.

'I should guess Mary, although she is distinctly distant with him. This seems odd, when they knew each other as children. Some misunderstanding, no doubt. The two young foremen are smitten also, they asked my permission only today, if they might call at the weekends. I must admit, they are both personable young men.'

'Of course, there is no comparison,' said Mrs. Stuart. 'Archibald is an educated young man with excellent prospects. I must tell Mary, she would be a foolish girl to turn Archibald down.'

Had they but known it, the same Archie was getting into deep water. He often brought small gifts of luxuries to Mrs. Stuart and the children. He ingratiated himself into the family circle.

Of course, Davie and Alan were disgusted that the Stuarts encouraged Archie's visits.

'That one is up to no good at all, Davie. Asi behaved strangely the other evening when you were over at Murdoch's flat. Archie arrived to tell me about an urgent order for Calcutta and, of course, I had to offer him a drink. When he tasted his whisky, Archie pulled a wry face and said, "I don't much like your whisky, Taylor: it has been well-watered." I did keep cool, with an effort, but said, "How dare you insinuate such a thing, let me taste it." Indeed it had little flavour. "Asi," I shouted, "what sort of whisky is this?" "From same bottle as yours, Sahib," he replied. Then, I told him, "Bring the Bottle!" You know, Davie, the whisky in the bottle was perfect. Asi assured me later that he had in no way interfered with the drink. We have had our bearers for nearly five years now, and you know that they are loyal and beyond reproach: but someone had watered the whisky. It transpired later that Archie had an ulterior motive in calling upon me. He said he was short of stores and could I lend him meat and cigarettes until the next order came up from Calcutta.'

'And did you?'

'With an ill-grace, I'm afraid. I could not help saying: "You should buy fewer gifts for the ladies, then you might manage to pay for enough tinned sausages from Calcutta".'

'I have heard that he has been borrowing food and money from several of the boys recently,' said Davie.

'But wait, you have not heard the worst. In a confidential whisper, he said: "I really came from kindness of heart, to warn you about your friend Davie. Don't trust him, he is a troublemaker, his whole family were a nuisance in Ruary: you know, of course, that we come from the same small village in Scotland".'

'I'll be damned! He really is after my hide now—perhaps because I'm in favour with Mary.'

'I'm only repeating this, Davie, to put you on your guard.'

'Did you answer that accusation?'

'Of course I did. In cold fury, hardly able to control myself, I said: "I think you can live without tinned meat and cigarettes, McCulloch— don't bother to come back EVER or I'll blacken both your eyes for you. Get out!"'

'So, Archie begins to show his true colours. He is trying to drive a wedge between us, Alan, beware, we have been warned.'

Davie called his bearer, Ram.

'Ram, I wish to know what happened to Mr. McCulloch's whisky when he visited Mr. Turner.'

'I beg pardon, sahib. I see now that it was disgrace for Turner Sahib. I was with my brother, Asi, and I heard all. It was the only way I could think to show anger. Asi is very cross with me.'

'Your anger?'

'He is a budmarsh. He has a very young Indian girl in the village— she is our cousin's cousin. My family is very angry with McCulloch Sahib, because he is very unkind to the girl and has hit her very often.'

'I see, Ram. This time I will overlook your fault, but on no account are you to do such a thing again. He was Turner Sahib's guest. That was disservice to Turner Sahib and to me.'

Ram was really troubled. He knew that a lesser man would have dismissed him on the spot.

'So, it begins,' thought Davie.

After his abrupt dismissal, Archie adopted more subtle ways.

One night, after dark, a machine-hand came to the Burra Bungalow and asked for Davie.

'Much trouble with paper breaking, sahib. Murdoch Sahib sends for you.'

'Take a driver plus sticks and lanterns, Davie, in case of snakes!'

'Whatever is wrong, Murdoch? Has there been an accident?'

'No, Davie, but the "stuff" periodically runs much too thin and the paper is breaking every few minutes. We have piles of broke and waste.'

'That's odd, Akbar is a good hand and a capable beaterman. Let's go to the beaters first!'

'Sir, I have mixed the same furnish—mixture of fibre and other materials—as always and added the same amount of liquid.'

The turning roll of the beater was drawing in the half stuff in correct quantity. The revolving roll was lying full weight, mashing the fibres. The water was being absorbed correctly but whereas the fibres should at the next point have been slimy to touch, they were much too wet— almost liquid—too wet to drain off properly on the great machine wire.

'Well, Murdoch, extra water has appeared in the after crush. There is no tap there, so . . . '

'My God, Davie, somebody has deliberately added water at the crucial point.'

'Yes. Well, we must just stop the whole machine, clear out this beater and reprocess. That will take at least fifteen hours. Now listen, Murdoch, you are not to give any reason for this to anybody. Just say "there was a breakdown". Keep your eyes and ears open, for this is sabotage and we must discover the rascal.'

It had taken two hours to locate the source of the trouble.

At tiffin next day, after Davie had told the manager of the incident, he said to Alan: 'Someone tampered deliberately with the half-stuff in MY beaters for MY machine. I would suspect McCulloch, but he knows nothing about papermaking.'

'Don't be naïve, Davie. He could have paid somebody to do it for him.'

'Well, it has to be one of the beater assistants, to know where to cause such damage.'

'Say nothing, Davie, we shall all listen and watch.'

After twenty hours, the beautiful, strong, white paper was rolling again. But the stoppage had been a loss to the company and was so far unexplained. Davie, usually slow to wrath, was inwardly fuming. The trouble was meant for him personally; it just had to be Archie.

One month later, in daytime, the paper colour suddenly changed to a mottled blue. The colourman swore that he had not added such a strong mix, only the usual small amount of blue to make the paper gleaming white.

When the third event occurred, Davie really saw red. Fortunately, it was quickly noticed. The guillotine knife had been reset and reams of paper had been cut to the wrong size. It could go back into broke, but time was wasted. The manager, Alan, Davie, the beaterman and machineman all had a meeting that evening. After long discussion, it emerged that the two native assistants on the beaters and the man on the guillotine were all related.

Ram and Asi were summoned.

'Do you know this family?'

'They are cousins of the Hindu girl of McCulloch Sahib.'

So, there lay the answer. All three strongly denied complicity but were dismissed forthwith. They did admit that they had spoken with McCulloch. The management was now forewarned. Mr. Stuart was the hardest to convince. He refused to believe such a thing of the suave McCulloch. There was no proof, Archie had become wily and very subtle.

'Now we know why Archie is short of money,' said Alan. 'He won't be quite so welcome either, at Shangri.'

So, Davie was exonerated. Life dragged on in the heat and the ladies departed for the hills, that hot season of 1908. Davie and Alan had six weeks near them in the hills and romance gave life a new purpose.

Mrs. Stuart knew nothing of the incident at the mill and continued, therefore, to be very pleasant to Archie, who paid particular attention to Mary.

'I think it is because we are such old friends, Davie, he wants to irritate you.'

'Perhaps also because you keep him at arm's length, Mary,' said Alan. 'He considers himself irresistible.'

'Alan, he is getting at me through Mary. I'm worried about her.'

'He's a real rotter, he now has two native girls in the village. If he is not careful he will get dysentery or cholera, or worse.'

Mrs. Stuart was a poor judge of character and voiced her displeasure when she at last sensed romance in the air.

'Remember, Mary, you are the governess of our children and, as such, you have a certain dignity to uphold. From this house you could marry well—an army officer in a hill station or a man with a bright future like McCulloch. He will have an excellent salary one day. Linda, you also should think of improving your future. When you return to Britain, you will no longer enjoy the advantages you do here.'

One Sunday, when Mrs. Stuart's emotions had developed from displeasure to anger, the girls were visibly upset. So, after siesta, Davie and Alan walked up to shangri and asked Mr. Stuart, *in loco parentis*, if it would be acceptable for them to ask Mary and Linda to marry them.

'Well, yes, of course. You are both eligible, hardworking and likely to do well in life. Speak to the girls.'

It was a late afternoon, never to be forgotten. Mary and Davie sat in the shade of the verandah, and Linda and Alan under a large shade on the lawn. Ayah was playing with the children.

'Mary, we have known each other for many years now.'

'Yes, we first met soon after you left the smithy.'

'Now I am twenty-nine, Mary, and for all these years I have loved you, even all the years we were apart. I thought of you when the lark soared or the thrush sang, or even when I walked by the Ripple—there has never been anyone else—will you share my life with me? I'm only a foreman, with little schooling as you know, but with your help I can improve my station.'

'Oh, Davie, I don't care what you are, I just love you for your own self.'

'You WILL marry me then, Mary?'

'Yes, Davie, I shall be honoured to.'

Davie gazed at her with those great, blue, honest eyes, then kissed her tenderly.

'You could marry a man with money and position, darling. I will never be able to offer you material wealth, but I love you dearly.'

'Dear Davie, ever since I found you again, I have hoped for your love—it seemed symbolic that after all those silent years you should have been waiting for me at Rawnpore station. I thought you would never ask me.'

'Mary, you are so very beautiful and so elegant. I felt you were too far above me—too good for me.' Then diffidently again: 'You really mean that you will marry me, dearest?'

'Dear Davie, I long to do just that.'

After a long silence: 'I would like to be married at home. The Stuarts return in a few months. I feel that I ought to return with them, because I did promise to take full charge of the children.'

'I am due home leave this coming hot season, so as soon as a replacement foreman comes, I shall follow you.'

They remained until dark. Linda and Alan also looked blissfully happy. Mrs. Stuart wished them happiness in a rather frosty way, but Mr. Stuart was delighted and the children rapturous. The young men were asked to stay to dinner and good wishes were exchanged all round over brimming glasses of cool wine.

Later, the Ekka was brought round and Davie and Alan were driven back to the Burra Bungalow. They spoke no word, just gripped each other by the hand as a silent goodnight.

6

It had been agreed that Mr. and Mrs. Stuart and the happy couples would keep news of the engagements secret for a week—until letters were well on the way to the girls' parents, to assure them that the young fiancés had been approved by Mr. Stuart, for in 1909 it was 'not quite the thing' if the prospective groom did not ask the father for his daughter's hand in marriage.

The Stuarts had decided to leave within the year—a new director was available. Little Margaret was so unwell, she was just fading like a flower, so they were anxious to get home as soon as possible.

Before Mary and Linda had received replies and good wishes from their parents, nearly ten weeks had passed. In the meantime, the two couples had paid a three-day visit to Calcutta, the girls chaperoned by the missionary's wife. It took two days to go round the many small jewellers' shops in the city, but both Mary and Linda found the ring of their dreams. Davie bought Mary a very beautiful five diamond ring—each diamond supposedly representing a word: will you be my wife?—and a most unusual gold bracelet with inset diamonds and turquoises. Dewy-eyed and lovely, she was speechless with delight, and treasured them all the days of her life.

To think that she, Mary Chisholm, a few years ago had been struggling with a milk-round and queuing at the butcher's late on a

Saturday night to buy, very cheaply, the meat which could not be kept until Monday morning. Very similar thoughts were passing through Davie's head. He saw himself as a ragamuffin, in a state of collapse outside the ragwash of the Ruary mill. It was incredible that Mary should be his fiancée and that, at that moment, he was able to buy her expensive jewellery in a Calcutta shop.

'Oh, Davie, can such happiness last?'

'Mary, we will make it last, come rain, come shine.'

All his life Davie considered that his Mary was 'special'.

The news, of course, had broken in their absence. When Davie left his beloved that evening at the Stuart bungalow, she whispered, 'Davie, we have completely forgotten about Archie. Do be very careful, won't you?'

The very name was like a cold douche.

'Don't worry, dear, I can sort him out all right.'

It was like waiting for a storm to break or for the rains to come, and when it did, it was a great relief—a sort of catharsis of mind and spirit, washing away all the fears, inhibitions and mental agonies of his youth.

With hindsight, he said, 'Alan, I shall never understand how one family could terrorise a whole community, the way the McCullochs did in Ruary. Perhaps because we were all so poor and so dependent on the laird employing us, and the laird considered McCulloch senior, to be a good ghillie.'

'Perhaps the McCullochs took good care that your laird did not know what actually was happening in the village.'

Later, Alan said, 'Now, Davie, no matter what vile words or insinuations Archie may make about either Mary or yourself, you must keep calm. Self-control is very important with an animal like McCulloch.'

Much more anxious than he would have admitted, Alan had spoken secretly to the two faithful bearers. 'Ram and Asi, you must speak to all the other servants and you must all be on the alert to protect Cameron Sahib.'

'We know, master—from McCulloch budmarsh.'

Alan looked surprised. He had forgotten about bush telegraph.

'Cameron Sahib is a very kind master, very generous, we look after him.'

Before dusk, thin wire mesh doors were always fitted into place, and similar frames into all window spaces. This allowed the maximum air in, but kept birds, small monkeys and snakes out. They were so near the jungle and were constantly aware of its dangers. It was commonplace for the servants to kill three snakes in a week, within the compound, especially where there were chickens. Very rigid precautions were taken at all the bungalows. It was all the more alarming, therefore, when a young cobra was found in Davie's clothes-cupboard. Because of the new protection being afforded his young master, Ram had moved his sleeping mat across the bedroom opening where Davie slept. In the night, Ram was awakened by a peculiar muffled sound. Lifting the ever-ready lantern and the forked stick, which were at the ready in various parts of the bungalow, Ram opened the door to the clothes-cupboard and there was the loathsome creature. Fortunately, Ram had his wits about him and yelled for Asi and other servants. Fortunately, also, it took the cobra seconds to rise before it could strike. Several people arrived and the angry cobra was soon dispatched. At daylight, it was found that two bricks had been removed from the outer wall section of the clothes-cupboard. Every pocket of every garment, every shoe and sock, was examined in case there might be scorpions or other vicious creatures secreted there. Finally, the whole cupboard was scrubbed out with carbolic to kill any eggs. The bricks, too, had been securely replaced. Ram was adamant that no servant at the Burra Bungalow would do such a thing, and especially not to Cameron Sahib. The whole affair was very upsetting, for it meant extra, trusted servants had to be on watch night and day.

Several days later, at breakfast time, Alan and Davie were kept waiting for breakfast. Finally, boiled eggs were brought in, instead of the usual tasty grill.

'What has happened to our breakfast, Ram? Did the other sahibs also have boiled eggs?'

'No, master,' said Ram. 'The other sahibs left earlier, you both came late from the mill.'

'So?'

'Well, master, Asi saw the McCulloch no-good cook going into our cookhouse. We caught him and he carried a plate with two fried eggs.'

'Yes?'

'He said that his master had no bacon and that he had sent his eggs to be fried in your fat to give them a flavour.'

'Well, I'll be damned,' said Alan.

'So, master, the cook and I threw away the sausages which were ready for you both, and the fat. We feared they might be poisoned—and it was so, your dog is very sick, master. I am truly sorry.'

Well, things had now gone too far. Davie's philosophy that 'the quietest way is the best' was shaken. Archie meant to get rid of him, one way or another.

Mr. Stuart was informed but, in utter disbelief, said, 'That is too much. I cannot believe that one white man would do such things to another, in a close community like Rawnpore. We all have to be friends here.'

The other white men rallied round. Alan and Davie were invited to eat at the table of any one of them—without invitation or request. No native cook, therefore, knew where they would eat. Stores were adjusted accordingly.

Perhaps to feign innocence, or to sound out the general feeling, or because Mary and Linda were departing with the Stuarts in a matter of days, Archie, insolent as ever, appeared at the Burra Bungalow one night. He was most unwelcome and nobody offered him a drink.

'Hmm, I don't seem to be wanted here!'

'No, I threw you out quite some time ago. Remember?'

'Head-foreman at the mill, huh, they must be hard up. I remember him'—using his thumb to indicate Davie—'he was a real rapscallion. The cottagers were all thieves and poachers.'

To be called a thief was the last straw for Davie. White with anger, he shouted, 'Enough is enough, Archie; you are a poor, soured, creature with venom in your veins instead of blood.'

'Don't imagine you will ever marry Mary Chisholm. I'll see to it that you never do.'

'Archie, you would do well to seek employment elsewhere because your die is cast, both here and in Scotland!'

'You devil, you won't live to gloat.'

'Gloat? Do not judge me by your standards. I tell you now, Archie, before these three witnesses, that if a hair of Mary's head is touched, or if anything nasty happens to me, you will be in irons, in a matter of hours. You see, I had the foresight to leave a witnessed letter in a bank in Calcutta, when last I was there, to the effect that, in the event of any mischief or accident to Mary or to me, you were to be the first suspect.'

'Huh! As though your word would count against mine! I have friends in all the right places!'

'Furthermore,' continued Davie inexorably, 'I have left in the same bank a second letter to be opened if the first was considered not valid— to the effect that you are guilty of attempted murder.'

The silence was nerve-racking.

'You are out of your mind. Hold him!'

'No, Archie, apart from all your attempts to discredit me in the mill, you have tried to kill me at least twice. I now have witnesses to prove it. That, however, is far from all. I was on the bridge at Ruary when you

93

pushed poor, pregnant Annie from 'Craigallion' into the pool—the deep one in the Ripple—I helped to pull her out. You may remember that, when the child was born prematurely, Annie died. All this is written and witnessed, and is available to the police. You stand irrevocably condemned!'

Seeing that Davie, by this time, was out of breath, Alan added, 'So don't try anything else on any one of us. Get out!'

Archie stumbled down the verandah steps. He looked white and podgy. Somehow his frame had shrunk. Davie even felt sorry for him.

'Phew! You didn't tell me all that, Davie.'

'No, I hoped he had changed his ways.'

'Is it all true?'

'Absolutely.'

'I don't see how he can remain here any longer, after that denunciation. The servants will talk.'

Nemesis was biding her time.

7

After one year, the Stuarts prepared for departure—with unconcealed relief by Mrs. Stuart, very mixed feelings by Mary and Linda, and excitement by the children, who were becoming bored by the necessary restrictions on play areas. Besides, it was more than time that Russell and Elisabeth went to school. Everyone was worried about Margaret, who became daily more like a little doll. The child never complained but was obviously very ill.

Privately, Mary and Linda agreed that the huge amount of luggage for one year had been excessive to the point of ridicule. The whole weary business of packing and labelling had to begin again.

Mary and Linda had bought a few gold trinkets, some Benares ware and some lengths of pure silk to take back as gifts. Finally, everything was packed and crated. Archie was not to be seen. Mrs. Stuart 'thought it a little strange that he did not come to say good-bye; he must be ill'.

However, Davie and Alan were there—torn between parting with their loved ones and pleasure that they would see them in a few months time for that very special date. Indeed, it needed both Davie and Alan to help Mr. Stuart to get the ladies to Calcutta, then aboard ship with their mountain of baggage.

'Let this be a lesson to us, Davie, when we are married. Let the rule be "Travel light" ', said Alan.

Too soon, they were waving farewell and with an ache in their hearts, watching the ever widening stretch of water grow between them. There was no delay in Calcutta. They had to get back to work.

The arrangement was, that Davie and Alan—who were due five months' leave, that meant a month travelling each way, and three months at home—would follow their prospective brides as soon as temporary replacements would be out from home. It was not possible to travel together. Alan, having been with the firm longer, went first; and about a month later, Davie followed. Alan and Linda were to be married in Yorkshire, Davie and Mary in Glasgow, which was the best centre—halfway between their respective families. Much, however, was to happen before then.

Indeed, Archie had not arrived to say goodbye to the Stuarts. Despite his discomfiture and the battle of words that day, on the verandah of the Burra Bungalow, Archie appeared to be his own, old, nonchalant self. Only Archie, the insensitive one, could have played it so cool. Not only did he have Premda, his young mistress in the village, but he had seen a lovely, dark-eyed young girl in the bazaar and had started to make advances to her. This was too much for Premda whom he had promised to marry, although this would have been frowned upon by her whole family. Her brother, head of the family, had frequently forbidden her to visit Archie's garden house, but Premda was infatuated with him. She was known, by sight, by many of the white men. She was a dainty little thing and as pretty as a picture in her colourful sari, her many thin gold bangles making a faint tinkling sound as she walked gracefully along the path, around the edge of the compound. One morning, she was making her way earlier than usual towards the garden house, because she was afraid. Her brother had threatened to send her to relatives, deep in the plains, out of the way of this budmarsh of a white man, if she ever saw Archie again. But she had to see him, she was pregnant, he must marry her soon, otherwise her brother would not even send her south as threatened, but would whip her and throw her out like a dog. So, on opening the garden house door, Premda was utterly stunned to find Shira, the beautiful bazaar girl, installed possessively in her place. She swayed and fell.

Archie, with incredible cruelty, merely said, 'You are too late, Premda, go away. You are no use now anyway.'

The lovely girl dragged herself home, wondering frantically what she could do. Nothing. The following morning, she was found dead. Her many relatives were distraught and more than suspicious. They soon found traces of a poisonous root in a drinking vessel beside her and came to their own conclusions.

According to the rites of her religion, her body had to be disposed of before dusk. So, the body of the young and beautiful Indian girl was carried down to the ghat at the side of the Ganges, burned, and her ashes cast on the waters before sunset.

Shira continued to seek Archie's company.

'I can't understand what these lovely girls see in the fellow,' said Malcolm. 'He must have some secret attraction.'

'Money.'

Feeling grew and surrounded Archie. The feeling of hate was almost palpable. His bearer rarely took his eyes from him, especially at meal-times. It was highly disturbing. He began to drink too much. Even the monkeys did not chatter any more. There were only these weird sounds from the jungle. When darkness fell, it was as though a sinister black vapour enveloped him. Too much whisky and too little food upset his stomach and his liver. He was squeamish all the time. Jaundice? It was difficult to get up in the morning, he stopped going to work, the dhobi no longer kept his clothes clean. Ugh! Whisky stains and tobacco ash everywhere. Archie tried to take a whip to his bearer, 'it was his fault', but he fell in the attempt and his servant did not even try to pick him up.

Now, he was afraid. He had never been ill in his life and all he wanted was to fall into bed. He was bathed in perspiration and was hardly aware that day stretched into night and night into day.

'Get the doctor, damn you! I've got malaria.'

Dr. Sim merely shook his head and said, 'Stop drinking so much whisky and go home on leave.'

'Old fool,' thought Archie of the doctor. 'I just need rest.'

He had no pain at all, he just became weaker and weaker.

Ten days later, he did not have strength enough to hold the whisky glass.

'Where is that bitch, Shira? She should be here to help me.'

His office acquaintances were puzzled. It was the complete disintegration of the white man. Archie just slept longer and longer until, finally, he just did not wake up at all.

The climate being what it was, his body was carried that same afternoon down to the burning ghat, where Premda's body had lain so recently.

About a dozen of his compatriots, among them Davie and Alan, watched the burning and then the ashes cast into the brown waters. This disposal of an acquaintance was harrowing to watch. The missionary held a short service. It was all over before the sun set.

'It is so sad, Alan, even with all his evil, to come to such an end. May God forgive him. I think he must have been ill in his mind.'

'I doubt it, Davie, he was completely amoral—just a clod of clay.'

Alan added, 'Someone, the assistant secretary or the manager, will have to inform his people and send home his personal effects.'

What difficulties some people make in life,' thought Davie. 'If we had had even the most distant of relationships I could have called on his parents and taken his things, but they would probably set the dogs on me.'

Enlightenment came from Ram when Davie said, 'How sad it is that a man should die alone, so far from his own country.' The usually kindly, loyal Ram looked hard at his master, saying, 'Not sad, Cameron Sahib—just. He was evil and had to die the way his Premda did.'

Davie looked in disbelief at Alan.

'Deliberate, Alan?'

'Yes, slow, painless poison I should say.'

Nobody mourned Archie, nobody regretted his passing. No happy memory of him remained. What had that human being achieved in life?—nothing but his own puffed up pride and self importance, an arrogance in physically subduing all whom he considered inferior. Davie kept on wondering whether there had been a soul there at all.

However, happier events were afoot. Both relief foremen arrived by the same ship so that, to their delight, the two friends could travel home together. They showed the new men round and were impatient to be off. They had left the option, as to whether they would return or not, open for six months.

'I'm really glad to be going home. Six years here is more than enough. Do you think you will return, Davie?'

'I doubt it, Alan, but we must find out what the girls think, and what the job situation at home is like. Meantime, let us pack up.'

8

Mary and Davie married at midsummer in the Crown Hotel on the outskirts of Glasgow. When the ship called at Malta, Mary had bought very fine hand-made lace with the Maltese cross clearly defined in it, and yards of heavy lace with the cross hand-worked in silk, also yards and yards of narrow lace suitable for underclothing and nightwear. Linda bought lace also. Both girls remained with the Stuarts at Maidenhead until replacements were found. Russell and Elisabeth were at day school, so no governess was needed. Margaret was very frail, her heart condition was becoming slowly worse. It was heart-breaking to watch the change in her. She was, however, perfectly happy and so obviously pleased to be in her own home again. They had said good-bye to Ayah in Calcutta. She had been a sweet girl and very intelligent, but she had no wish to sail to a cold country, so far from home. Mary and Linda had been sensible in not spending much of their money in Calcutta. They had bought the souvenirs for their friends and families, when they were in Calcutta with the boys. They felt that there was enough clutter without buying more. Finally, Mary arrived in Port Glasgow after eighteen months absence. Only the two youngest children were still at school and Fred was doing the old 'family milkround'. The dairymen used to joke and say that their trade would finish when there were no more Chisholms to do the round.

Frank was now a qualified ship's engineer and was on a trip round the Cape to Australia. Jane hoped he would be back for the wedding. Dick had been apprenticed to a cabinet maker and had his father's clever fingers. Tom had started work in a shipping office. Fred, at fourteen, had just started an apprenticeship in a ships' engineering shop.

Mabel and Ethel would be Mary's bridesmaids. Mary made her own wedding dress of pure silk and Maltese lace. There was a band of heavy lace around her waist and from bodice to hem at the front. There was a high boned neck of very fine lace with matching sleeves. It was exqui-site and she felt it looked much too fine for her.

Jane looked years younger. Her childbearing days were over and she was always so neat and tidy, but there was silver now in her dark hair.

She would look nice in the grey silk Mary had brought for her and the bridesmaids would be lovely in the dark rose.

George and Jane had moved to a large flat on the gound floor. They had an extra bedroom and a larger kitchen. It was still not big enough, but it was the best they could afford. They still had the lovely view, overlooking the Firth.

Meggie had written to Davie and to Mary, saying that they must consider her home as theirs—until they had one of their own. She knew how cramped they would feel in Port Glasgow. She would be down to the wedding and they could have a chat then. Meantime, Mary had accepted the offer of a good neighbour, that Davie should have her spare room until the wedding.

In no time, it seemed, they were awaiting Davie's arrival. It was wonderful, the ship was coming to the Clyde and would put passengers ashore at Princes Pier. What could be more convenient?

George and Jane, of course, had not met Davie but, from all accounts, he seemed to be a fine chap and Mary was a sensible girl, they were sure she would choose well.

Father thought it weakness in a man to show emotion, but he was obviously delighted to see Mary and gratified that she had come home to be married.

'So, Father, I would not find a husband if I went into a family as a governess, eh? Take it back.'

'I might, when I see the lucky fellow.'

Davie, with his quiet, gentle ways and his fair good looks, soon became a great favourite with the family. As always, he was over-generous. All his life Davie had never counted the cost to himself—he would always see the other person right. Now, Mary was aware that he was spending far too much money on all of them. She had to whisper frequently, 'Don't be over-generous, Davie. Remember that we have to live for months without pay, then find work.'

This was a theme all through their married life. As a young bachelor, if he gave away too much, then he did without himself—until his wage packet appeared. Mary was well aware, from her early childhood, that there had to be some sort of budgeting. She quickly took charge of the family purse. She learnt, also, not to admire anything in a shop window—or he would go in to buy it, before she could stop him. Apart from Sarah and Meggie, and for a little while his mother, he had had no one to love him, and Davie himself was so full of love all the days of his life, he could never do or give enough wherever he was. Mary loved him dearly, but had to be the practical partner.

99

The great day dawned. Mary, her mother, and her bridesmaids stayed over-night with Flora-Dora, to their great delight. Davie, George and the boys travelled to Glasgow by an early train. They were such a happy wedding group. Frank's ship had docked the previous week and he was acting as best man because Willie, Davie's brother, had not been sure that he could come.

Alan and Linda, too, were absent. They were too busy making their own preparations, but their telegram arrived on time.

Davie and Mary had eyes only for each other. Mary was so beautiful and Davie so handsome in his Cameron kilt.

There was great hilarity and a fund of stories at the wedding breakfast, but the bride and groom were happy to escape at the earliest opportunity. The guests were going on to the music hall later.

Nobody had been told where the young couple meant to go, they just disappeared under a hail of rice and confetti, in a hansom cab, picked up a suitcase from the left luggage and boarded the train for Tarbert and Loch Lomond.

There they stayed one night and caught the morning train for Fort William. The weather was perfect, clear and sunny, the mountains were mirrored in the lochs, the deer were grazing by the side of the railway—showing no fear.

It was idyllic, they were blissfully happy and felt complete and fulfilled. Each wondered how life had been possible, alone and apart, for all the years. One hot evening in Rawnpore, Mary had described to Davie her trip to Arrochar with the aunts. When she expressed a longing to go all the way to Fort William, Davie had whispered, 'How about honeymooning there?' 'Nothing could be more wonderful. Think of the cool, green hillsides and the tumbling waterfalls,' said Mary.

In that torrid area of the plains, heaven itself could not have sounded more beautiful. And here they were, man and wife, in the little West Highland train, just passing the great moor of Rannoch.

It was a minute or two before they were aware that the train had stopped. It was a single track, there was no station, so they were curious, opened the window and looked out. The moor was a lonely, forsaken area but as Davie leant even further out he saw a tiny cottage—just a but and ben—by the side of the railway. Mary squeezed in beside him to find out what was happening. An old man in an ancient kilt stood in the doorway and the train driver was shouting to him:

'Has that retriever of yours had her puppies yet?'

'Aye, five.'

'What colour?'

'I'll show you.'

A middle-aged lady in the next carriage also had her head out the window.

'Good man,' she shouted. 'We have paid a lot of money to get to Fort William this night, not to collect livestock for you.'

The driver took no notice.

'I'll have the all-black, McNab. I'll collect it on the way back tomorrow. I'll need a saucer and a can of milk for it.'

'Right, bring us a basket of fish and some groceries from Fort William.'

As the train moved slowly forward, quite by accident two lumps of coal fell from the tender.

Mary and Davie were convulsed with laughter.

'Where in all the world would a driver hold up a train and all its passengers to examine a puppy by the wayside?'

'Only on the Moor of Rannoch,' she answered.

It was all one to them, when the train would arrive in Fort William. Tomorrow was as good as today.

'It is incredible, now after Rannoch, the scenery is still more spectacular. I really did not know that such beauty existed, Mary.'

She said nothing, just slipped her hand into his.

So the golden days passed. They travelled from Fort William to Oban. Oban Bay in the moonlight had to be seen to be believed. The steamer trip to Mull and to Iona was superb. How they loved each other! Such bliss should never end, but, of course, it did—but not yet awhile.

PART III

I

After the honeymoon, Mary and Davie had decided to go to Meggie's for most of their leave. They went firstly to Port Glasgow to pick up their belongings and then went north. There were rooms to spare at the farmhouse. Peter's parents had retired and moved into the cottage, so Peter and Meggie now ran the farm. 'Linaird' was the farm but, in the area, the farmer was known by the name of his farm. Instead of being called 'Munro' he was Linaird. There were acres of rich arable land, as well as grazing for sheep and cattle. At the end of the kitchen garden was a neat, white, two-roomed building—the bothy—where two farm-hands slept, although they ate in the farm kitchen. It was harvest-time and all hands were needed from dawn to dusk. Local farmers helped each other the day that the 'threshing-mill' arrived. This enormous creation moved from farm to farm in the area, for the number of days required to thresh the corn and the barley. Wheat was not successful in the area.

Meggie and Mary baked and cooked all the hours of daylight. Davie was the go-between, he carried food and ale for breakfast, for mid-morning, for dinner, for tea. Then all the men, who had come any distance, came into the great farmhouse for supper. Neighbouring wives also helped in the kitchen. The mountains of food consumed had to be seen to be believed. Davie thrived on it. Both Meggie and Mary agreed that they had never seen him look so well. And still the cows had to be milked, calves and chickens to be fed. Great bowls of milk had to be set out in the dairy, after evening milking, so that the cream could be skimmed off in the morning—that meant butter to be churned. The cycle never ended.

Davie and Mary, in the early morning, learnt to have a spoonful of porridge, then a spoonful of cream from a separate bowl. They decided that this really was the life. What sort of life was it in Bengal, struggling to make a living at 110° + in the shade?

When the harvest was in, and the threshing done, they really had to

decide what to do next. This farm was such a happy home. Meggie and
Peter were so well matched, so fortunate in having the farm and, with it
all, two lovely children, a boy and a girl.

Davie and Mary were sincerely delighted for Meggie—she deserved
it all. Despite all the work, she was a home-maker. It was so cosy in the
evening, sitting in the lamplight, mending clothes or darning socks,
that India was but a memory—another world. It was really only at this
period by the parlour fire, that Mary and Davie realised what a return
to India would mean, especially a return to Rawnpore, that near-jungle
village with few comforts.

'How would you like to rent a croft and learn to work it, Mary?'

'I'd love it, but we would not get very far on the proceeds. Besides,
we have no money and no experience.'

Meggie said, 'You really have to be brought up to work the land,
Davie, it would take you years to learn.'

Then again Davie would say, 'You are aware, Mary, that if we return
to Rawnpore, life is going to be very different for you. At 'Shangri',
with the Stuarts, you lived in luxury, and in quite a big family circle. If
we go back now, we go to one of the small bungalows near the Burra
Bungalow. We could only afford a bearer, a houseboy and a cook.'

'I have been thinking about that, Davie, and also that there might be
no Linda and no Mrs. Logie. Gracious—will I be the only white
woman in Rawnpore?'

'Surely not, but changes are rapid in that place.'

Davie had been receiving copies of the 'Paper Trade Review' sent
each month. He had been astonished to find very few jobs for foremen,
advertised. Of course, he had been out of the 'home circle' for nearly
seven years now, and posts were often not advertised. The news of a
coming vacancy was passed on verbally. In a sense, he had to become
known again, if he were to continue in the trade in his own country.
Two months leave had passed, there was only one to go.

The pros and cons were discussed each evening, and they were each
aware that the other did not wish to return to Rawnpore.

However, the decision was made for them; for a much delayed
telegram arrived one morning. It had been sent to Mr. Stuart, who in
turn had sent it to Port Glasgow and, at last, it was forwarded to
Linaird.

'Manager ill, urgently request David Cameron's immediate return
to Rawnpore.'

So, it must be said that, in sadness, they drove the gig to Ellon and
sent a cable.

'Mr. and Mrs. David Cameron will return as soon as possible to Rawnpore, for one year only.'

They both agreed that one year was as long as they could suffer the heat. They had to pack up and depart for Port Glasgow within days. A happy letter from Alan and Linda was awaiting them there. Their situation was similar to that of Davie and Mary. There was nothing doing in the trade, at the moment, and they wondered whether Davie and Mary would be interested in going back to Rawnpore for two years, to save hard and return home for good. A 'wire' was sent to Alan and Linda that Davie and Mary were returning on the first of October, for one year only, by the 'S.S. Adora' sailing from Princes Pier, Greenock. The Post Office was kept busy. Two days later, a reply telegram was delivered with the one word 'Agreed'.

Too soon they were aboard, but to their great delight Alan and Linda boarded the 'Adora' in Greenock also. The trip out was uneventful and quite pleasant, but the girls found that travelling in a second class cabin for two, even with a porthole, was vastly different from the suite of cabins they had previously enjoyed. Both girls were resourceful and uncomplaining. Indeed, Davie never knew how claustrophobic Mary found the cabin at times.

At least they had no nightmare over luggage, for there was only one cabin trunk and two in the hold. There were the high moments also, and there were those glorious moonlit nights in the Mediterranean when they just could not leave the deck. In the Red Sea, they slept on a chaise-longue on deck.

When things became dull in the Indian Ocean, the chief steward, who had fallen for Mary and openly regretted that Davie had got her first, said, 'Don't say no, because it is your birthday tomorrow and we must have a cake and a party to liven this dull lot up.' So, much to their amusement, there was cake and champagne and a rendering of 'Happy Birthday to You'. They made a few shipboard friends, exchanged addresses, but never saw them again. Three days in Calcutta to pick up stores, silks and muslins and, in no time, they found themselves back in Rawnpore. The girls' arrival this time was somewhat different. There was no reception committee, just Malcolm, the machineman, to welcome them back—but in the ekkas outside sat two beaming bearers, Ram and Asi.

The manager and his wife were in the hills. He had been too ill to travel home but their belongings were still there, so Malcolm regretted that Davie and Mary would have to live in one of the small bungalows near 'Shangri', and Alan and Linda in the other one.

Mary and Davie agreed later that this was a good thing because there might have been 'feeling' if Mary had been installed in the manager's bungalow while Linda was in a smaller one.

Davie just had to ask Malcolm the question which had been trembling on all their tongues.

'Who has come as the new secretary?'

'A very nice fellow from Bristol—Simon Marks by name. As different as chalk from cheese, from the last one.'

Only Davie and Alan had heard the word 'poison' uttered, the others thought that McCulloch had just drunk himself to death. It was inevitable that the subject would still be under discussion.

'You know,' said Malcolm, 'we were all saying just last night, that it was odd how McCulloch changed from an arrogant young bastard to a drunken lout in just a couple of months. He seemed to go to pieces all at once.

To change the subject, Mary said, 'Malcolm, we went to see moving pictures in Glasgow.'

'You mean a magic lantern.'

'No, indeed. Pictures in which the people walked, ran, danced.'

'You mean the pictures flowed one into the other?'

'Yes, but only for a few minutes. It was fascinating. We had to pay threepence to go in.'

'Well, Mary, you will still have to make your own fun in Rawnpore, but it's great to have you back, like a star in the night.'

'That's enough of that, Malcolm,' said Davie. 'Anyway, when are you going to bring a wife out yourself?'

'I'll have to decide next visit home.'

2

So life went on, but not as before. There was still the heat and the dust, and the long weary hours in the machine-shop. Most of the faces were the same—a few new native employees but, of course, life now held more meaning for Mary and Davie.

Alan and Linda had been allotted a bungalow of similar size on the other side of the compound. This was an excellent arrangement. Although they were intimate friends, it took a little effort to visit each other, thus granting greater privacy. However, the girls made a point of meeting each day. Davie and Alan met at work or in the evenings. The relationship was still as close, but different.

Ram looked after Mary's comfort in every detail. It took time to learn how to manage the servants, Ram really ran the household, but Mary was very observant. The day might arrive when there was no Ram Singh on whom to rely. She and Davie had brought gifts for Ram, his wife and children, and Linda had done the same for Asi. Ram's gift had been a clock, of which he was inordinately proud.

Mary had also brought back a sewing-machine, not too big. It had a strong handle to turn on the right-hand side, but best of all, the whole machine had been made rust-proof to withstand the humidity of the area. It had been pounds dearer, but as she said to Davie, 'What is the good of a rusty machine if I am sewing white silk?'

The greatest surprise of all, they kept secret until the welcome back party. After drinks and food had been served, Davie slipped into the next room, leaving the communicating doors open, and suddenly there was the most delightful sound—quiet at first, then soaring to a wonderful crescendo—it was the glorious, golden, tenor voice of Caruso.

The excitement was enormous. Davie displayed several wax cylinders. Everyone peered down the horn, but nobody was allowed to touch it. The difficulty was going to be, keeping a box at a suitable temperature so that the wax remained unaffected.

'Leave Mary to wind it, her fingers are more delicate.'

'Then if it breaks it will be my fault.'

'As though I should ever blame YOU for anything. I would say it had been kutcha'—makeshift.

They had cylinders recording songs, dances, classical music, even one of music hall jokes.

The extravagance had been worthwhile, it was giving pleasure to the whole community. There was this same attitude throughout their married life. They were forward looking, alert to progress.

Linda, too, had brought a sewing machine, so, in the comparative coolness of early morning, the two girls had sewing sessions together.

'My father said that, one day, everything would be electrical. He saw an electric iron in an exhibition in Glasgow recently.'

'Roll on the day,' said Linda.

Mary was the letter writer. She wrote long letters, describing their daily routine in detail, to her mother and to Meggie, and when the replies came two to three months later, they were read avidly over and over again, in silence, then aloud to each other. Every detail from home mattered so much.

'Davie, we won't stay too long in Rawnpore, will we?'

'No, darling, we shall go home for good after this year. This experience which I am having as "acting manager" is well worthwhile and will surely mean a better post back home. It would be a good idea, Mary, if your father bought and sent us one of the "Paper Trade Reviews"—just to see how things are moving.'

They now had their own ekka to get about—to the bazaar, to visit friends, to have short outings. Ram was most careful to check all corners and cupboards, as well as their section of the compound, early each morning for snakes. When they wished to drive along a section of the river, Ram would say, 'Be careful, Sahib, while you were away, a man-eating tiger killed a boy in the next village. He has not been caught yet and his tracks have been seen near the river at Rawnpore. Always carry your gun and your snake-stick.'

That was something else that Alan and Davie had learnt to do, while in the Burra Bungalow. After tiger tracks had been seen within a few miles of the compound, and after terrified natives had refused to walk near the woods, because they claimed to have seen a king cobra on the path, Mr. Stuart had insisted, during his last months in office, that all the men connected in any way with the mill, must learn to use a gun. A range was set up and every man had to practise there twice a week.

This season had been drier than ever and the wild animals were coming openly to the river to drink.

'It is really quite a performance going for an outing on a Sunday,' wrote Mary to Meggie. 'I have learnt to handle our horse but Davie forbids me to go out alone EVER. So there we are: Davie and I in the first ekka plus gun. Then, in a second ekka are Ram and another servant with snake sticks. Imagine what it is like when Alan and Linda are behind with their outfit. You won't be surprised to learn that we are always home before dusk.'

Then one Sunday morning, as they drove down to the river just for a very quick breath of air before breakfast, Davie and Mary actually saw a huge Bengal tiger drinking at the edge of the river. Mary had pointed a trembling finger, saying, 'Look Davie!'

The horse pricked his ears and stopped dead. The tiger was about one hundred yards away and they were on a narrow road. Davie had to get down and, with much soothing and clapping, induced the terrified horse to turn in the narrow road. Just as they drove away, the tiger lifted its head and gave them a long enquiring look.

'He must already have had his breakfast,' whispered Davie, trying to be cheerful.

On their return to their bungalow, Ram was standing on the verandah looking very anxious. His worry, for the first and only time, made him forget his position. 'You one damned silly sahib to go driving alone on that road. Tiger not forget you,' and he turned and walked away.

Feeling suitably chastened, they sat down to breakfast. Mary was visibly shaken. Neither of them realised that the strain of living so near the jungle was getting on their nerves.

The incident had to be reported, of course, at the Burra Bungalow, where a warning bell was rung. As the inhabitants of the compound appeared, a warning was shouted to one and all. 'Carry your rifles to work! All others must remain inside the bungalows!' For the first time, Mary felt fear in these surroundings. Alan brought Linda over, and both were warned on NO account to leave the bungalow. Three days later, the tiger was shot on the edge of the native village. Only then did anyone relax.

Now that Archie had disappeared for ever, Mary and Davie settled into an even tenor of existence.

Mary said, one evening, 'All this happiness is too good to be true, Davie.'

'Don't say that, Mary, life is just evening itself out, we had a rotten childhood.'

'We must, I suppose, expect some difficulties, but remember we always have each other. I still pinch myself wondering whether you really are here with me.'

'I'll pinch you hard enough to make you sure.'

Life did, inevitably, become more difficult.

Davie's old stomach trouble started up again. Mary kept him on a light diet. He lived on chicken soup, and milk puddings, but obtaining milk in sufficient quantities proved difficult, so they bought three goats and things were better. Of course, he was under considerable strain—acting as works' manager, starting up a new type of board paper on one of the machines, and just coping with the heat generally.

Then one night, in the glow of the sunset, Mary whispered that she was expecting a child. After a long pause, when Davie could control his voice:

'Would you like to go home, Mary, perhaps to Meggie's?'

'Are you trying to get rid of me already?'

'No, my darling, but you will find the humid heat unbearable, we are so near the swamps.'

'You can take me to the hills and stay three weeks, then fetch me in the autumn and stay another three weeks. If I don't go farther than Darjeeling, the separation will not be so bad. The baby will be born early in November.

'Then, for the birth, you had better go to Calcutta, to have the child in the hospital there.'

'Do you really believe that the doctors there are any better than Dr. Sim, who trained in London?'

'No, but ... '

'He delivers the native babies, when there are difficulties.'

Davie, who did not want her so far away, agreed.

Dr. Sim said he would like to have a trained nurse come up from Calcutta, and:

'Would it not be a good idea if you wrote to ask Mrs. Stuart's former Ayah to come and help with the baby afterwards?'

'My mother had ten children, Dr. Sim, and managed without all that fuss.'

'Maybe, Mrs. Cameron, but this is Bengal, and this particular area has special difficulties, as you know. You cannot possibly cope alone, and Ayah Ria already understands the difficulties of conditions and climate in Rawnpore.'

When Davie came in, he affirmed what Dr. Sim had said.

Alan and Linda were wonderful friends. As soon as Alan heard that Mary was going to the hills for three months, he most unselfishly said to Linda, 'Would you like to do the same?'

So, for nearly three months, Davie and Alan were alone again, except that they accompanied their wives to Darjeeling and stayed three weeks, and fetched them home again in September.

Ram carried out Mary's orders about diet for Davie, most faithfully.

So, the men struggled through the heat and the work and the dust; 'coming up for air' as Alan said, when they went for the girls.'

November dragged on, day by day, and Mary became anxious, but Dr. Sim said quite simply, 'It does not matter how you count, nor how often you count dates, Mrs. Cameron, the baby will not come until the moon is full. In Rawnpore we count by moons not by calendars.'

Finally, after a long, protracted and agonising labour, Mary's baby was born—a girl.

Davie was ecstatic and gazed at mother and child in rapture. This sheer delight in his wife and child never left him. This baby was beyond his comprehension. Although his youth had been spent among babies, none had appeared so angelic. How he would work to support them! How he would educate his daughter, yes educate, for he knew full well how much pleasanter it would make life for her.

Davie's daughter was baptised in the tiny mission church by Mr. Beale, and given the names Alison Sarah, but all the servants called her Beti Baba—baby girl. She was the first white child to be born in Rawnpore. Alan and Linda acted as godparents and the whole community spoilt her shamelessly.

Alan, however, noticed amid all the excitement, that Davie grew thinner as each day passed and was not surprised, therefore, when he collapsed in the hot machinehouse one morning. Dr. Sim had him sent to the hospital in Calcutta, he was in such pain. It was a blessing that the steamboat, which brought woodpulp down river, was going on to Calcutta that afternoon. It saved Davie a long, hot, dusty train journey. Alan could not be spared, so Murdoch, the machineman, accompanied him and saw him settled in a cool room in the hospital.

Mary, naturally, was distraught. Alison was only three months old and, therefore, she could not be left even with Ayah. Dr. Sim made her eat sago twice a day, to retain the flow of milk under stress. He was a great believer in sago and was convinced that was the secret of the native women, who could always breast-feed their babies.

Ram was the perfect bearer. When Mary insisted on remaining in her own bungalow, he brought in his sister, Maya, to help. By great good fortune, a telephone had just been installed between Calcutta, the jute mill and the paper mill—but not in the bungalows.

Alan, who was now acting manager, telephoned several times a week

from the mill to the hospital and reported faithfully to Mary. Mary
sent letters by the ships' captains, who, if they had time at all, went to
visit Davie in Calcutta. So, there they were, each worrying about the
other. Davie remained in hospital for six weeks. He had stomach
ulcers, but they did not operate. A specialist from London was studying there for a year; he was writing a thesis on the effect of strong
curries and spices on stomach and liver. He had a long chat with Davie
and said he would advise long rest and light diet only.

Mary coped very well until Ram's father died. A relative arrived at
midday to inform Ram, Asi and Maya that their father had died that
morning. He had no other sons, so Ram said to Mary: 'Most humbly,
memsahib, does Ram ask pardon. My mother is alone. Asi and I must
go to have our father cremated before sunset. We shall return at
sunrise. It is too dangerous to travel after dark.'

'I am very sorry about your father, Ram. You will come back when
you say?'

'Ram gives his promise, memsahib. Another bearer will come from
the Burra Bungalow for this one night, to look after you.'

Indeed, Mary heard the temporary bearer being well instructed; also
that Ram would be only two koss away—four miles—and drums would
tell him if all was not in order.

All went well, until Ayah burst into her mistress's bedroom, while it
was still dark. When she awoke, all that Mary could see was the whites
of two large eyes, gazing through the mosquito net. The lamp was not
lit. Ayah then gasped, 'Memsahib, there is a snake in the hall.'

Petrified, for a few moments Mary seemed dumb. Then she grabbed
Alison, climbed onto the low bed and screamed, and screamed, until
the temporary bearer and houseboy arrived with lamps and sticks. The
young cobra was not killed quietly and efficiently, as Ram or Asi would
have done, but with much noise, shouting, banging and running about.
All this, meant that the gardener on duty at dusk had not done his
snake-round of their section of the compound, and that the temporary
bearer had not made sure that the wire mesh was firmly fixed in the
doorway, nor had the houseboy trimmed and filled the lamps—an
Indian household unsupervised.

The damage was done. Mary's nerves, so troublesome in her childhood, got the better of her. When she could stop her teeth chattering,
and the baby crying, she ordered the now contrite bearer, to bring the
ekka round. In her dressing-gown, with Alison in a silk shawl, she
climbed into the vehicle, followed by Ayah and the two servants
carrying the usual lamps and sticks.

At daylight, she arrived at Alan's bungalow and just fell into Linda's arms.

Dr. Sim arrived and gave her some laudanum. Alan sent a message to the works, that he would be very late and, after a great deal of pressure from Dr. Sim and her friends, she drank some tea and went to bed. She awoke a few hours later, and had a long talk with Alan and Linda. At last, she said:

'Linda, I have a great favour to ask of you. Would you and Alan permit me to stay with you until Davie comes home? Ayah, Alison and I could all share one room.'

'Why yes, of course,' Linda was saying when Alan broke in:

'No, Mary, that is not wise. Ram and Asi returned, as promised, at sunrise. With the two bearers, Murdoch and I have searched your bungalow in every nook and cranny. The cupboards have been washed out and all your clothes searched. We have gone over the grounds inch by inch and there is absolutely nothing to be afraid of, now.

If you do not go straight back to your own home you never will, and what would Davie do?'

Asi will sleep on your verandah and Ram will sleep in the hall, across your bedroom door. Dr. Sim advises this also. He will give you a sleeping draught and Davie will be back in a few days.'

She was a sensible girl and, although highly apprehensive, she agreed.

Ram was beside himself with anger and grief. He hoped the mem-sahib would understand that he had to go to his father's cremation.

'I have thrown the gardener out of the gate, and I have personally taken great pleasure in kicking that budmarsh bearer down the steps of the verandah.'

Mary could not help smiling to think of those bare toes kicking anybody. Later, she heard that he had even pursued the offending bearer all the way to the Burra Bungalow, thrashing him with a stout stick.

In a week, Davie was back, pale and thin, but better. His diet was a problem. The meat from the local bazaar was tough and stringy and it had to be soaked in a solution of Condy's crystals to disinfect it. Even when thoroughly washed, it had a peculiar flavour, to say the least, and Davie could hardly be prevailed upon to eat chicken.

After his return from hospital, they had a month together in the hills and they both felt better.

In the cool of the hill-station, they had a long talk. Rested and cool they could see things in perspective.

'Davie, you have now worked in Rawnpore for more than seven years, don't you think you have taken this punishment long enough? We only came for one year, you remember. Let's stick to that and give your six months' notice. The longer you do the work—and on a foreman's salary—the slower the London office will be, in sending out a replacement for the manager.'

'You must hate the place, after your terrible experience while I was in hospital.'

Mary shuddered, 'Yes, Davie, I fear for your health and for Alison's safety, apart from my own experience altogether.'

'You have to consider, darling, that, even if I were to find a head-foreman's post, we would have to take a big cut in salary—and no perks; that has to be compared with the life we have here.'

'If you are asking my opinion, Davie, I would much rather be financially poor in the Home Country than comfortably-off in Rawn-pore. We can manage with a great deal less—just think of Alison being able to run in a meadow without us having to search every part of it for snakes!'

'Yes, this life is possible for a bachelor, but definitely not for women and children.'

She snuggled up to him and whispered, 'We know what it is to be poor, Davie. Don't worry, we could manage.'

On their return to Rawnpore, Linda had a meal for them. Ram drove them over to Alan's bungalow and the conversation soon turned to the crucial question.

'Well, Davie, are you and Mary of the same mind still? Because Linda and I are.'

'Absolutely, Alan, we leave as soon as we have completed the year promised.'

'Right, we can give notice to the office tomorrow and set things in motion.'

Linda put into words, what was in all their minds:

'It is really only the perks that are good—not the salary. You are both half-killing yourselves for a pittance.'

The others were astounded, it was not often that Linda voiced an opinion in such a decisive way.

Mary added: 'Conditions seem to get worse and, between going to Calcutta and the hills, we are certainly spending much more than we intended.'

'Something else worries me a lot,' said Alan. 'These past two very dry seasons are bringing so many wild animals down to the river. In the eight-and-a-half years I have been here, I have never seen so many. Hyenas raided the broke store at the mill last week.'

'It isn't really a place for our wives, Alan, and certainly not for Alison.'

They gave notice of a maximum six months, with the proviso that they be allowed to leave two weeks after replacements arrived. The very thought of returning home, for good, removed all their fear and depression.

Laughter and the joy of life returned. They had their lighter moments.

Mary and Linda would sit on the verandah, sewing, chatting or playing with the baby.

'Look at your little dog, Mary. I do declare he sits at that spot on purpose, to tease the hanumans.'

'Yes, that big monkey sits on the lowest branch of the mango tree and moves its long tail backwards and forwards as slowly and deliberately as possible. Jackie tries to catch it—there now, listen to that shriek. If the dog catches and nips its tail, the monkey gives poor Jackie such a clout it sends him flying right over to the verandah. Jackie never learns.'

'Do the same monkeys remain here all the time? Can you tell them apart?'

'Oh yes, they are individuals all right. Look at that little dark one over there! When I am here alone, sewing, I have to wave to her, otherwise she comes over and peers around the pillar and knocks until I look up. When I say "Hello, Mirza" I swear she smiles. Davie says I must be careful not to become too friendly—she could become jealous of Alison and hurt her.'

A few days later, Mary was shocked to find Alison very flushed and restless. She sent for Dr. Sim, who affirmed that she had all the symptoms of malaria. She seemed to make a good recovery, but three weeks later the baby was ill again. The shivering fits lasted longer, she was constantly sick and, one awful morning, Mary noticed that soft, rosebud complexion had gone and her baby looked distinctly jaundiced. Dr. Sim looked grave and said to Davie:

'The child is very ill. She is suffering from intermittent malaria and is jaundiced. This is the worst possible area for her. I advise you to send your wife and child back to Britain on the first ship sailing from Calcutta, otherwise the child will die.'

Consternation throughout the community! The recently installed office telephone proved a godsend. The 'S.S. Horda' was sailing in one week and, again by good fortune, was continuing from Southampton to the Clyde. No steamer was available, however, from Rawnpore. Linda was upset and did not wish to be the only white woman in Rawnpore, so Alan suggested that she pack a trunk and leave with Mary. Davie was grateful, Linda would be such a help to Mary.

'This has been one devil of a year, Davie. I think we were not meant to come back.'

'I can't hold out much longer myself, Alan. We must hope that replacements come soon. Perhaps an urgent message could be sent to the London office.'

A first-class carriage was booked for the four of them. Dr. Sim gave Mary what medicine he could and told her to report to the ship's doctor at once.

There was a temporary hold-up before the Empress Hotel would admit them. Fortunately Dr. Sim had given Mary a certificate to the effect that the child had jaundice. However, the Health Office at Embarkation insisted on examining the child. Fortunately, her temperature was not very high at the time and he issued another certificate 'Jaundice'.

The firm had managed to book a large first-class cabin, which all three shared. It was airy and had one of the new electric fans.

Within the week, therefore, the young couples were separated; there had been no time for long, fond farewells, there had been too much to do.

'Thank God for you and Linda,' said Davie, 'we would never have managed without you.'

'Linda has been very nervy since Mary's experience, while you were in hospital, so it has all worked out for the best.'

'Alan, we have just time, before our train leaves, to send cables. I shall cable Mary's parents to meet her in Greenock, you had better ask Linda's to go to Southampton.'

It did not even occur to the young husbands that their savings were depleted because they had to pay first-class expenses for their wives. Had husbands and wives departed together, this would have come under their Agreements with the firm.

Davie and Alan slept during the slow train journey back to Rawnpore. They had wasted no time in Calcutta, because friends were working extra hours to cover their absence. They slept in their own bungalows but ate together at the Burra Bungalow, as they had done before they married.

'Mary and I had decided on our last home leave, not to return to

Rawnpore, and were just about to write and tell you so, when that damned telegram arrived. I'm sorry if we influenced you and Linda in making up your minds.'

'We were so undecided and had no job, so we might have done it anyway.'

'That is generous of you, Alan. We would have been in a sad state here without you this year.'

'It is easy to see what we might or might not have done, with hindsight. Let us just look forward to getting home as soon as possible.'

The two friends spent their free time getting packing cases, selecting what they would take home and what they would leave.

One evening, they chatted about Asi and Ram. They had been most faithful servants, indeed they had become friends and the long years they had spent in their service must be recognised. In conversations during the past seven or eight years, the two brothers had always talked with longing about a strip of ground in the foothills—a strip which they could cultivate together, where they could build two mud houses for their families, apart yet near enough, to be happy.

Davie and Alan could see that the heat of the plains was telling on the physique of Ram and Asi also, and they obviously dreaded going into service as bearers to other families. The kindness of Davie and Alan, through the years, had been returned in full measure. The young white men made enquiries of the district officer as to the price of a piece of land, small but yet large enough to support two families, near the foothills, where the earth was good and the climate pleasant. The price was within their means.

So that the bearers would also have something small and tangible, they sent to Calcutta for two inexpensive watches. Ram and Asi had been extremely honest throughout the years and they had made sure that all the other servants in the house respected the white man's property. This certainly could not be said of all bearers in the compound. These gifts and certificate of land ownership were handed to them the night before departure.

Tears of gratitude ran down the cheeks of the two native bearers; they could find no words to express their feelings, they salaamed repeatedly. But the extraordinary thing was, that the bearers also had a surprise for the sahibs. From the pittance they were paid, they had managed to buy in the bazaar two tiger's claws, tipped with a tiny gold ring so that they could be hung on a watch chain. They were truly gifts of affection. Davie and Alan were overwhelmed.

'They must have saved annas for a very long time to buy these,' said Davie.

'Or perhaps their cousin's cousin in the bazaar sold them at cost price.'

'It is just as well we have our eight years' bonus due to us, Alan.'

'Yes, we must watch our cash very carefully from now on.'

Three-and-a-half months later, they stood on the ship's deck, watching Calcutta slowly disappear from view. They had absolutely no regrets about leaving Rawnpore. Davie had spent nearly eight years there—a whole slice of his young manhood toiling in that hell-hole—but he had found his Mary there. He had been meant to go to Rawnpore. Now, it was a changing community. Soon the miracle of electricity would transform life there, with gadgets and advantages beyond their wildest dreams.

Mary had remained in Port Glasgow. She had taken the neighbour's room, next door to her mother. George and Jane had been waiting for her as the ship put the passengers ashore at Princes Pier. Jane had expected to welcome a beautiful, rosy-cheeked, fair-haired child and was shocked to see a thin, jaundiced scrap of a child, with sad blue eyes and no smile.

'Don't worry, Mary. She will be all right now.'

At the earliest opportunity, Mary took Alison to a specialist at the Sick Children's Hospital in Glasgow. He prescribed a very strict fatless diet, to which Mary strictly adhered. It took years to get over the malaria and the jaundice.

3

Davie and Alan parted in London. They tried to be brisk and formal, but both felt the sadness of the parting. It seemed the end of an era, as indeed it was. It was 1911.

'Now, Davie, do write, this address will always find us. We must keep in touch.'

'Of course, Alan, good friends are precious. Meggie's address will always find us.'

A firm handshake, and they parted.

Twelve hours later, Davie was hugging Mary as though he would never let her go, and there too was Jane, holding Alison. He gazed at his little sallow-faced daughter, with straight flaxen hair, and thought she was the most beautiful child he had ever seen. He would not let her go and carried her to the waiting cab. Mary and Jane brought his light grips. All the trunks and packing cases were being sent direct to Linaird, where Meggie would take charge of them. There was no room in the Port-Glasgow flat.

'Alison looks much better, Mary. I have been so anxious about you both.'

'And I about you, Davie!'

They spent a week chatting, walking out in the cool sunshine, even in the rain—gazing at the clear water of the Clyde and the beautiful green hills of Argyll. They walked for miles, pushing Alison in a little pram, it was so wonderful just to walk out on the spur of the moment, without fear, without servants, without snake-sticks.

'I lift my eyes to these hills every morning, Mary, and thank God for you and Alison.'

Then later, 'We cannot live in one room much longer. How would it be, if we took a little house at the coast, over there round the Holy Loch, not too far from your family, just for the summer?'

'Oh, Davie, it would be wonderful, let us take the steamer over tomorrow to Kirn and we can ask locally whether any small houses are to let, furnished.'

'I must order a "Paper Trade Review" regularly now, to see what jobs are on offer. I cannot afford to be idle after the summer—our money will just dwindle away.'

Mary more than agreed. She was the practical one.

'You must not be over-generous, Davie, we now have no income, no perks, no free holidays, so we must be sensible. It was just as well you had no time to buy gifts for everyone in Calcutta. We brought everyone handsome gifts last time we came home. I could keep the house on two pounds weekly, Davie, but if you gave me two pounds and ten shillings, I would put the ten shillings into a bank for household emergencies.'

In the weeks to come, Davie was somewhat shaken to find that there were few opportunities for foreman's work offered in the "Trade Review". He had been head foreman for two years and acting manager for a few months in Rawnpore, but he would be happy to settle for a foreman's post.

'You see, Mary, I have been out of circulation for the past eight years. Nobody knows me and the better jobs are often offered without being advertised. I have to get into the stream somehow. I need a good referee who knows me personally.'

'Then why not Mr. Stuart, he knows you well?'

'Good grief, why didn't we think of him months ago?'

Davie was just about to accept an assistant foreman's job in Northern Ireland, when the new copy of the "Trade Review" was delivered and there was an advertisement for an assistant manager in a four machine mill in northern Aberdeenshire. He applied, they waited on tenterhooks for the reply. It was slow in arriving, but did request him to go north to be interviewed.

He returned with mixed feelings to talk things over with Mary.

'I was offered the job, Mary—it is a big mill, in excellent condition. They make all types and grades of paper there, but there are two snags. One is, that the owner's son is the manager and it is obvious that he draws the salary and I do the work; the second, that they are offering me a pittance of a salary—three pounds and ten shillings weekly, with a rent free flat and lighting. The flat is fairly near the works and has electric light from the mill's own generator.'

'You are tired, let us sleep on it.'

Next day, they discussed all the pros and cons.

'The choice really is this, Mary—a lot of responsibility, at least a twelve hour day, very little money—but wonderful experience in all grades of paper, vellum, parchments, coated papers, newsprint—the lot.'

'You could not stay under these conditions for always, Davie. You must at least receive a decent salary for the hard work.'

'Perhaps after one year, I could have an increase, if you think we can manage in the meantime.'

'We can manage; for dire emergencies we have our tiny nest-egg from Rawnpore.'

They were installed in the flat by Christmas. They had bought easy-chairs, a mahogany table and sideboard, and some bedroom furniture at a local sale. It was the first time they had ever made bids at an auction.

As Davie learnt to know the mill, so Mary learnt to know the range in her kitchen. No matter how she coaxed the fire, it gave little heat and the oven did not appear to function. So, she started at the beginning by getting in a chimney sweep to clear the chimney. He was a decent fellow and started to clean the flues for her. They were absolutely blocked—had not been cleaned for years, he said. After his efforts, the fire roared, the oven heated and it was bliss. When properly treated, it was a wonderful little range. On one side was the oven and on the other a tank which heated water to almost boiling point. A brass tap at its base released the hot water as required. It was important to keep the boiler full of water—but what a blessing for baths, and clothes and dishes!

'Davie, do you know what causes me most work in this flat?'

'Alison?'

'No.'

'Cooking?'

'No.'

'What then?'

'That range, but I'm not complaining. It is the best thing in the flat, and I wouldn't be without it, but after the flat has been warmed up, I let the fire get low, then out come the blacklead and the emery paper and the bathbrick, then I relight the fire, heat the water, have a bath . . . '

'Oh, stop, Mary, does it go on forever?'

'I'm only joking, darling. I'm truly happy.'

It was true. She never made comparisons.

Davie said, 'I feel so inadequate. When I married you, you were a beautiful young lady, living in luxury, with servants to wait on you and now, after a couple of years, you are down on your knees, cleaning out filthy old flues.'

'Davie dear, you know quite well that the young lady period was a mere front. We are both workers and I'd rather be here with you than anywhere else.'

She truly was 'special', thought Davie. She could always cheer him up when he felt depressed.

Alison was improving daily, and was very active. After an exhausting morning, she was glad to have her after dinner nap—then Mary sat down at her sewing machine and produced incredible things. Warm winter coats made from remnants, heavy curtains to keep out the draughts, shirts, underwear—she made the lot. She turned skirts and jackets, added a piece of braid—and had new garments.

They were so happy and so thankful that Alison was recovering. Her skin was sallow now, the yellow had faded. Each Friday evening, Davie laid three whole, and one half, sovereigns on the table and Mary glowed. They were poor, but it was not the grinding, abject poverty of their childhood. What they could not pay for, they did without. On fine Saturday or Sunday afternoons, they walked along the banks of the Law, which was bordered with lovely old trees—beech or fir, or spruce. To amuse Alison, Davie started to practice his bird songs again. When the snow came, he made a small sledge for her and pulled her along the paths and the sideroads. She was a contented child, quiet and obedient. They were a happy family unit.

The second year, they were in Inverlaw, the next blow fell.

Davie collapsed at work and was rushed off to hospital in Duncross. This time they did operate and removed the ulcerated section of his stomach. Poor Davie, his stomach had troubled him from his early childhood. The doctor assured Mary that he would be better than he had ever been, but henceforth he would need more meals and smaller ones. The firm had been good and paid Mary the golden sovereigns for the weeks he was off work. On his return, he thought the flat was beautiful.

'Your nimble fingers have transformed the place, Mary.'

As soon as possible he returned to work, dutifully eating the plain biscuits and drinking the warm milk which Mary provided.

'I can't take these, Mary, and eat in my little box of an office!'

'Do it for Alison's sake, and mine,' she pleaded.

Three months later, after overwork and a heavy cold, he started coughing up blood. Mary was petrified, she believed there was no cure. She had seen a young woman in the village, who lived in a little revolving wooden house in the garden—fresh air was the only cure, it was said.

But the old country doctor was more cheerful.

'Nonsense, lassie, all he needs is rest and good, plain food. Think what he has been through—you have told me yourself—unremitting toil since he was ten years of age, long hours in the heat of the Indian plains and now a fiendish Scottish winter, and in and out of a hot machine-house. Let him rest for a month or two.'

'Maybe the firm is mean with the salary, Mary, but they have been kind in continuing to pay me. This is the second illness within the year.'

They had clothes and to spare. Mary bought small pieces of choice meat and fish. Every morning, the milkman left sixpence worth of cream. This was poured over his porridge and over his favourite sago. He went back to work after two months, part-time.

They had had no chance to make friends. They had had to cope with so many difficulties, but the butcher, Ross, had been well aware of the situation. He realised that the choice meat was expensive and it was unusual to have choice cuts every day. He was a lonely widower, about ten years older than Davie and, learning that they were newcomers and alone, he went to visit Davie. He was the same type as Alan and they all took to him at once. In no time at all, he was Uncle Ross, to Alison.

As soon as he was allowed out of doors, Ross took Davie for rides in his van. He delivered meat to outlying farms, and Davie got out into the open country. On half-days, Mary and Alison were also squeezed in. 'Again,' thought Davie, 'I find a friend when I am in need.'

Mary tried to repay him by inviting him to Sunday dinner each week. Despite his own sadness, he was full of fun and, for his part, it was a joy to be one of such a happy family.

One or two of the machinemen came to visit him. 'Wish you were back, Davie. That b...... doesn't know what he is doing. "Do this, do that." He hasn't a clue when the slightest thing goes wrong.'

Donald, one of the foremen, brought a large piece of felt, enough to make heavy blankets for two beds. 'It is a good felt, Davie, it was only on the machine for forty-eight hours, so it is really new.

Felts were expensive items. They were made of wool—and were endless. They travelled, pressing against the wire, to pick off the stuff of the paper and carry it through the first press, getting rid of the water. The paper was carried on the felt between the great rolls, the bottom one with a rubber covering and the top roll often of granite or heavy rustproof metal. These rolls squeezed out the water from the paper stuff and the water ran through the felt and down off the perforated roll at the bottom. Then the paper was strong enough to continue, through the further rolls, itself.

These heavy felts were much sought after by the workforce, in mill and in office. Even after long service, the felt was still desirable for blankets but the longer it was on the machine the less pile it had. Happily for the owners, it was very seldom that a practically new felt was damaged or torn. They were so desirable that a good manager would keep a list of names of those wishing to have a section. A felt could be divided into quite a number of sections. Those at the top of the list received a section big enough for a large double bed, for a nominal sum of money. If the felts were well worn, the workers could have lengths for three shillings to five shillings. If the felt was almost new, therefore soft and with a long pile, a nominal ten shillings and sixpence would be paid.

A fair-minded manager made the men take whatever grade or quality was available when his name came up to the top of the list. Just such an excellent felt became available that week. Donald's name was at the head of the list and he had obtained enough for two double beds for fifteen shillings, which was a large proportion of a weekly pay-packet.

Soon after Davie had arrived in Inverlaw, this Donald had been suffering from a poisoned arm—and was in no state to be at work. He was in dreadful pain, the arm had to be lanced and dressed, and he was attempting to 'do his shift' because he needed the money—no wonderful penicillin then, no antibiotics available, just sheer misery. Davie had sent him home for a week and had gone to the owner to request that Donald be paid. He was a fine machineman and irreplacable.

It seemed that Donald had not forgotten the kindness.

'The wife agrees that we have enough felts, we still have good ones from five years back. We wondered if you, being ill, and not used to the cold here, might need them.'

Davie and Mary were delighted. Being 'new', even as assistant manager, he had hesitated and decided not to put his name on the list yet.

Mary insisted on paying the precious fifteen shillings, but it was the best bargain she ever had. The little green jug from the shelf would be empty again.

'Are you quite sure, Donald—you might never have the chance of such good felts again?'

'Quite sure, I've been in the mill for thirty years, our family have all the felts they can use,' and, shuffling out the door, he turned to Davie, saying, 'You're the first boss who ever helped me in a fix.'

'I'm so thrilled, Davie, there is enough for the double bed and the single, and for a heavy coat for Alison. It is a beauty, not an oil mark on it. We don't even need to dye it—only the bit for the coat.'

She blessed Donald many a time in the years to follow.

4

It is months since we heard from Alan and Linda. I wonder how they are faring?' said Mary.

'According to his last letter, Alan is having difficulty, also, in finding congenial work.'

Indeed, Alan had decided to take the work available—he too, was an outsider as far as the trade went. He and Linda had settled in Yorkshire, in the next village to Linda's family. In the 'Trade Review' Alan had seen an advertisement for a traveller for a wire firm—paper trade wires—and he was lucky enough to get the job. 'Lucky enough' maybe, but it meant that he was away all week, sometimes over the week-end as well, and it made both Linda and himself unhappy. They, too, hated to be separated. It also was to be a temporary post. He worked south of the border, so he did not call at Davie's mill. He was well paid, but it was a tiresome job, with long, slow train journeys and cabs between stations and mills.

But, nine months later, he did see his friends, the Camerons. Davie had recovered. The doctor assured him that it had just been a 'warning' but Mary made sure he had as much rest and good food as possible.

The year was 1914 and the month December, when the telegram was delivered. Mary shuddered, but all it said was: 'Arriving in Duncross 6 p.m. on Thursday. Alan.'

Davie managed to go in to the station to meet the 6 p.m. from Edinburgh. There was Alan, and Linda too, all smiles, but—Alan was in khaki. It seemed that he had been in the Territorials for the past six months and was now on leave before going to France.

Davie was aghast, but said nothing before Linda. They caught another train to Inverlaw—that was only a twenty-minute journey—and they arrived tired and hungry to a warm welcome.

Alison was still awake, so they had to have a peep at their goddaughter. Of course, she did not remember them, but gave them a shy, endearing smile. The sallowness was now disappearing and her lank fair hair was showing a delicate wave—she was becoming attractive again. After a good meal, they sat down to talk.

'Well, this is wonderful,' said Alan.

'Yes, but aren't our circumstances different?'

'We have a tiny rented house also. We both knew when we left Rawnpore, Davie, that we should have to "come down to earth".'

'Yes, but it did not occur to us that it would be so difficult getting back into the trade again. I'm very fortunate, being in such a good mill, but the money is very poor. If it were not for Mary making all our clothes, we would be in queer street; do you know, Alan, that when I was off for three months, she unpicked an old suit, bought good material in town and made me a complete three piece suit. You'd swear that it had been tailor-made.'

'That was the first and last, old boy—I blame that for my grey hairs,' broke in Mary.

'Guess what I'm doing!' said Linda.

'No idea!'

'I took a three months' course at a Post Office Centre in York, and I'm going to run a small village post office, together with the sale of sweets and tobacco in Oakley. There is a flat above the shop, it is ideal.'

'Well,' said Alan, 'we talked things over. I had absolutely no prospects in the trade—after all those years of toil and sweat too—so we hit on this idea of working together. I was with the Territorials, I considered it a good organisation for discipline and training, and of course we were the first to be called up when war was declared.'

'Nobody thinks it will last long,' said Linda.

'Let's hope not,' said Davie, with a faraway look in his eyes.

'Not having seen you for such a long time, we took this opportunity before I embark for France and before Linda opens the post office. I hope you don't mind?'

'Of course not, we are delighted,' said Mary. Her brain had been working furiously and she had decided to take up Ross's offer, which was made when Davie was so ill. 'If you wish any of your friends or relatives to come up, Mary, they would be most welcome to use my spare bedroom.'

Ross arrived about seven o'clock, as he so often did on Thursday— his half-day—so the matter was easily arranged.

'At Christmas, we had a post card, in a childish handwriting, from India. It merely said, "We are happy, many greetings" and it was signed in the same hand "Asi and Ram".'

'We did too, and wondered whether it was written by one of the sons,' said Mary.

'Strange, isn't it Alan, that they own a strip of India and we don't even own our own home?'

At the week-end, they walked along the riverbank, skimmed flat stones across the surface of the pools to count the rings, gathered great quantities of pine cones to help to eke out sticks, and fed breadcrumbs to the hungry birds. It was a winter idyll, which passed all too quickly.

'Alan, if you have the chance to send us a card, please do! Linda, we shall be anxious to hear about your new venture, so do write, please!'

They were off, as suddenly as they had come.

Davie had, of course, shown Alan round the mill. He was extremely interested in the vellums and parchments; he recognised that the wire had come from his previous firm, but he had no real regrets at having escaped from the trade and the long, weary hours of frustration it represented. He had worked in factories since he was seven years old, and really looked forward to being his own master when the war was over.

'Well, Davie, I can see the work and responsibility you have here and I think they have a b..... nerve paying you only three pounds ten shillings weekly for a mill this size, plus a finishing house with all the female labour as well. Don't be soft, Davie, ask for an increase.'

Six months later, Davie did, and was given four pounds ten shillings, but by that time he was grateful to be in essential industry at home.

He had been called up in the autumn of 1915, but, with his recent medical history, had been declared C3 at the examination. On the one hand, he was sorry that his health was deemed to be so poor but, on the other, very thankful that he need not depart to fight and to kill. Mary was greatly relieved. One week in the trenches in France or Belgium would have killed Davie. German shells and snipers would not have been necessary.

They had one card only, from Alan. In her last letter, Linda had expressed worry because she had not heard from him for so long. But in 1916, after Verdun, she received a letter to say he had been wounded and would arrive at a hospital near Oxford in two weeks' time. When notified of his arrival, she went down and was alarmed to see his head bandaged and a cage over his feet. Thank God, he had not lost his sight, but he had lost his left foot. He was later sent to a hospital in Derbyshire and, when he could walk with crutches, he was sent home. His war was over. He was thankful that he had a 'Blighty' and that he was lucky to be home again.

'Davie, you have not had a break for six months. Couldn't you take a few days to visit Alan in Oakley, he has no relatives—just Linda.'

It was extremely difficult to get away and the journey was slow and frustrating, but he arrived unexpectedly and the way Alan's face lit up at the sight of him, was ample reward. He could not hide his emotion. Linda, too, was grateful for the visit.

'You will cheer him up no end, Davie. He is depressed now that he is trying to get about, and sees his limitations.'

'I got a few of the bastards before this happened, but I sure am glad to be back. Davie, it is pure hell out there in the trenches.'

Mary and Alison had had a week at Linaird with Meggie. Peter, also, was working under difficulties. His two young farmworkers had been called up and he had girls helping on the land. Three of his five horses were requisitioned, his sheep and cattle were counted and registered, and the farm produce could only be sold through official channels.

Meggie knew that Davie needed all the nourishment he could get, so she had the joiner make a large wooden box with divisions in it—to hold four dozens eggs. This box was dispatched by rail once a month to Davie and, to the credit of all railway staff, it never ceased to arrive. There were a lot of honest people about, for many of them must have been tempted and the little lock could have been broken so easily.

Ross, or anyone at the works who was ill, benefited also from the delivery of fresh eggs.

Bread became grey in colour but it was amazing how often three white scones, three white rolls or a small packet of pure white flour, would be handed to him without a word. Davie was always amazed when people were kind to him, he could never understand why.

They spent as much time as possible in the fresh air, walking for miles each week-end—farther and farther from the village, until one day they came upon a little croft tucked away between the river and the woods. Being thirsty, they asked if they might buy some milk. The Calders were elderly and thinking of giving up the few acres they worked.

'Our son was killed this year on the Somme.'

They asked the Camerons to stay to tea; they were lonely and wanted to talk. Out came fluffy white scones and white bread, well buttered. They would accept no money and asked all three to come as often as they wished—in summer they had tea in the old-world garden and in winter around the fire in the cosy kitchen. Mary tried to return the kindness by sewing for them. She made warm flannel shirts for Mr. Calder and skirts and blouses for his wife.

'Isn't it lucky, Davie, that I learnt to use a needle?'

Even the war ended. It had seemed as though it never would. No more young men marched gaily past their windows, following a pipe band playing rousing tunes—on their way to entrain. No more Zeppelins flew over their coast-line, blacking out Duncross and stopping all trains. Even Alison remembered having to be carried on Davie's shoulders for seven miles one wintry night, when they had been turned out of a train because there was a Zeppelin overhead. The many young men who did not return were mourned, the few who did were fêted. There was, however, a lightening of the spirit again, a little laughter, a burning of black-out curtains.

Much to the disgust of Mr. Calder and many other farmers, Summer Time was kept. This extra hour, conceived in 1916 was adopted for every summer. Dear old Mr. Calder knocked on Mary's door one day, asking if he might wait there, until it was time for the next train to Duncross.

'I was in good time, I can't understand it. I'll be late for market now.'

'Well, dear, you DID refuse to put your clock forward, and Davie did warn you that you would forget the new time in Summer.'

She said no more, not wishing to recall to him the rare show of temper he had shown, because 'the government had dared to tell HIM what to do with his clock' . . . and much more.

One beautiful sunny Sunday, Ross had said: 'Now that Alison is getting bigger, there is very little room in the front of the van. Why don't you buy a bicycle.'

'A bicycle?'

'No, I don't mean a new Raleigh safety bike, I mean a motorbike.'

'A MOTORBIKE?' gasped Davie.

'Yes. You are tied to the village. It would do you good to get out and away. You could even travel cross-country to visit Meggie and come back the same day.'

'I wouldn't dream of buying a motorbike and of leaving Mary and Alison at home.'

'As though I would suggest such a thing. Yesterday, I was at the showroom in Duncross and I saw a bike with a large side-car plus hood and windscreen. There was plenty of room in it for Mary and Alison and a good windscreen for the driver, too.

Davie was always alert and willing to try something new, and Mary was right behind him.

'But, Ross, I've read that you have to run and push a motor-cycle to get it to start. That would still be a bit too much for me, especially with a heavy side-car. What a pity!'

'How about coming into Duncross with me, all three of you, next

Saturday afternoon, in the van? I don't want to raise your hopes, but I think, only think, there is a new gadget on this model which starts it.'

'And the cost?' asked Mary.

'Well—it is eighty pounds. Petrol is now ninepence a gallon.'

The four set off in the van as arranged.

'Wonderful, but frightening,' thought Mary her brain working feverishly on the money question. She and Davie had talked late into the night about this motor-cycle. 'Pros and cons again, Davie!'

'We could visit Meggie—there and back in one day.'

'We could have picnics in the country and hear the birds sing.'

'But the money, Mary—eighty pounds. At a pinch, if I was out of work, we could live a year on that.'

'Davie, we still have the two hundred pounds I saved when we came back from Rawnpore. I was keeping it for a rainy day. Don't you think that we have had a lot of rainy days, these past few years?'

'It would certainly open up a whole new world to us, Mary. We could even travel to Gourock on holiday!'

'Let's be devils, then—grossly extravagant. We can live on porridge and cream to make it up.'

'Mary, words fail me, you are such a good sport.'

So, in high glee, they went to the Lea showroom in Duncross, and there it stood in all its splendour. Pale almond green, very enticing. Friend Ross said not a word, just looked at them.

The salesman was talking:

'No, this is the new 1919 model—post war—you don't have to run to start it, unless something is far wrong. It has this side-kick starter.'

Ross knew that they were hooked, he just walked around with Alison to let them think.

'Eighty pounds! How Davie had sweated and toiled in the jungle heat to earn that. He deserved the bike,' thought Mary.

Across the showroom stood a new shiny model of the Ford Car—at one hundred and forty pounds, and a beautiful Humber.

'Look at that, Mary. One day, you will ride in one.'

It was a foregone conclusion. It would have been sheer madness to spend one hundred and forty pounds on a car, when they could have this for eighty pounds.

'What about the dust, Davie, for your chest?'

'Oh, I can wear a muslin mask across my nose and mouth. Anyway, the main roads are being tarred, now.'

The salesman said he would register the motor-cycle for them. It was agreed that they would return the following Saturday, pay for it and collect it.

'We had better come by train then,' said Ross, 'and I'll drive it home with Davie in the side-car. Mary and Alison can go back by train.'

'We don't need to come in.'

'You must be at the buying of it, Mary—our first motor transport!'

They had two wonderful years with their motorbike. They went up to Balmoral and along Deeside, or followed the Don to Meggie's. Ross would often accompany them for picnics—he now had a motorbike as well as his van. Sometimes, they would stay overnight at Linaird, when Mary and Alison would look after the farm on Sundays to allow Meggie and the children, or Peter and Meggie, to have a run to the seaside. After a taste of this freedom, it did not take Peter long to buy a car, one of the new 'Tin Lizzies'.

The ugly head of jealousy reared itself among some of the villagers.

Why should some people go jaunting about the countryside enjoying themselves, when others had to stay at home—and on the Sabbath, too. They failed to notice that the Camerons attended Church as often as anybody.

5

Davie and Mary had now been in Inverlaw for eleven years. They had good friends there, but in the post-war years were finding it increasingly hard to live on such a poor salary. There was not even the pleasure of seeing golden sovereigns any more, these had been withdrawn in 1914.

'You know, Mary, I feel we shall have to make a move soon or we shall never be able to educate Alison and save for our old age, we wouldn't eat very well on seven shillings and sixpence a week. There will never be a better salary for us here.'

This time, there was no need to answer advertisements. At a Trade Meeting in Duncross, Davie was approached by a tall distinguished figure, who held out his hand and said:

'You are David Cameron, I believe?'

'I am.'

'I'm Reith of Bervie, and I am looking for a competent manager. Mine is only a two-machine mill and I hear that you are in charge of four machines at the moment.'

'True,' said Davie, 'but I am very interested in a change.'

'Well, you would be in full charge of the works, but I fear I could not pay you more than seven pounds per week—with free house, coal and light, of course.'

It took all Davie's self-control not to say: 'I'll be there tomorrow.' Instead he said, 'May I come and see the mill at Bervie?'

'Of course, shall we say next Tuesday, about 11 a.m.?'

Well, he could not get home quickly enough to Mary. As soon as he saw her, he blurted out: 'I think I have got another post—as outright manager of a two-machine mill—at how much do you think?'

'Well, I hope at more than four pounds ten shillings.'

'Seven pounds plus house, coal and light—I can't believe it.'

'Well, dear, it just proves how very underpaid you have been all these years.'

'I did know that, Mary, but you remember I had to get back into the trade, then the war was upon us and I would not have been allowed to move.'

'Don't let us get too excited, until you have seen the place, Davie.'

'I've got a great idea. If it is dry weather, keep Alison off school for the day and you can both walk around Bervie, have lunch somewhere, and I'll meet you again about four o'clock. The bike is going to be very useful.'

'That would be a real treat.'

Bervie was a bustling market town and the mill was after Davie's own heart. It was three miles from the little town, clean and tidy, and it lay by the side of a silvery river. It made, mostly, expensive rag papers—but there was some variety. The watermark was 'Moonbeam'.

Early in the afternoon, Davie had shaken hands on the deal and asked if he might fetch his wife from Bervie, to show her the house.

'Delighted, of course. It happens to be empty.'

The house was perfect—a three bedroomed house, with bathroom and toilet. Even the washhouse and coalhouse were under cover—and the house was built of great blocks of gleaming granite. Round the corner was a garage and the whole was set in a good garden—flower and vegetable, and as far as the eye could see were fields, trees and the vital river.

The old sparkle appeared in Mary's eyes.

'It is the nicest house I have ever seen. It is even lovelier than Ruary.'

'We need you as soon as possible, Cameron.'

Davie need only give a week's notice but he intended staying a month, to allow Inverlaw to find a successor. The owner was so shattered when Davie said: 'I'm leaving'—so unusually angry, that Davie did indeed go in a week.

'You can't leave us, Cameron, you have been here so long, we thought you would stay for good.'

'No, Mr. Findlay, not at four pounds and ten shillings, weekly, for the responsibility I take. You have taken advantage of me, throughout the war years, when I could not move.'

'What salary are you being offered at Bervie?'

'Seven pounds with all the extras—including coal.'

'Well now, because you have been here so long, we could also offer you seven pounds, Cameron.'

'Too late!' Mr. Findlay. 'Too late!'

'I would have been furious if you had accepted it, Davie, after all these mean years,' said Mary.

'I'm not that foolish, Mary. Here there is only a primary school—at Bervie there is an academy, like Blairton. This offer has come just at the right time, Alison is now eleven.'

'Davie, when things seem so perfect, I'm always nervous. It all seems too good to be true.'

They moved into the new house at the end of January. The weather was clear and crisp, frosty at night and in the morning, with beautiful sunny days. Alison remembered exactly what these two weeks were like, they were etched on her memory for ever. After these two weeks, the most testing time ever came for the Camerons, and Alison left her childhood behind her.

They had had many trials and tribulations since their marriage, but now they were, in very truth, put to the test. Two wonderful, happy weeks in their new home, then the agony. Again, it was poor Davie who became ill.

At the very mention of acute abdominal pains and semi-consciousness, the doctor arrived post-haste from Bervie in his new Ford car. Within the hour, the ambulance was on its way back to the same Duncross infirmary, where he had already been a patient, and the Bervie doctor was worried enough to accompany his patient the full twenty miles to hospital. The diagnosis was—peritonitis in an advanced stage. There were no hope-giving drugs, like penicillin, no sulphanilamides, no streptomycin—just the frail body and iron will-power of Davie Cameron, who wanted to survive.

Although Davie had only managed the mill for two weeks, he and Mr. Reith had become friends. They were two of a kind, the only difference was the material one of cash and possessions. Mr. Reith could have quite justly, for the times in which they lived, have dismissed Davie and engaged another manager, for Davie was to remain in hospital for more than three months. Instead, he took over the job himself and paid Mary, the full salary, regularly each week. In other ways, too, he proved a tower of strength. In his Humber, together with Mary and Alison, he followed the ambulance to Duncross.

They all waited until the long operation was over to know whether he would survive. They saw him still unconscious from the blessed chloroform, back in bed and with a cage across his middle, for he had several tubes protruding from him.

Mr. Reith drove them home in sorrow, and that night, Mary had to draw on all her reserves of spiritual strength to survive until morning. This night, Alison found hers.

Each day, Mary walked the three miles to the station, travelled to Duncross to visit Davie, then did the return journey. It was an ordeal. He hardly knew her, and the lovely blond curls were streaked with grey, the blue eyes clouded with pain. On the Saturday, she and Alison went together. They found the bed screened off and a stern sister saying, 'the child is to remain only five minutes'.

Davie looked at Alison and said, 'Who is that? Send her away!'

Shocked, she was led away to wait in the corridor, and her long wait instilled a fear of hospitals into her for ever.

It was Saturday afternoon, yet young nurses were scrubbing the floor of a side ward. Screams came from the children's ward opposite, Alison felt abandoned. At last, a doctor was accompanying Mary from the ward, saying: 'You are not on the telephone, twenty miles is too far away, without transport, you must live in the hospital while your husband remains in this critical condition—but not the child, of course. You must send her home.' And he strode away with Olympian aloofness. They were both stunned. Stay in hospital, just as she stood? Send Alison home? Where?

'Let's go out and have a cup of tea,' said Mary.

Seated at a small table, with steaming cups of tea before them, Mary continued: 'This is what we must do, Alison, we have no choice. I have very little money with me, I did not mean to do any shopping. Therefore, we must go to the police, explain the situation, ask if they can lend us the money for your fare to Glasgow. I shall send a wire to Grannie to have someone meet you there, at the train. I'll put you in care of the guard. You must stay with Grannie as long as is necessary.'

A large sugar bun lay on Alison's plate, but she could not touch it. Great, slow tears ran down her cheeks but she said nothing. The only fact which registered was 'He did not know me, he did not know me!'

A tall, severe-looking woman, who was sitting in the corner, never took her eyes from them—most rude, Alison felt. Indeed she was so embarrassed at the unremitting stare, that she turned her tear-swollen face the other way. After a time, this seemingly disapproving figure got up and swayed towards them.

'It is obvious that you are in trouble? I feel that I can help you. Do you care to tell me, what is wrong?'

Mary swallowed hard and told the tale.

'You will do no such thing as going to the police, nor must you send the child away by herself. My name is Gordon. I live in the manse in the next village to Bervie—about seven miles away—and the child will just come back and stay with me; my daughter is about the same age and will lend her clothes. We have no telephone, but we will contact the police officer each evening to have news of your husband. Here is my card. Contact us when you return home.' This was the point when Alison learnt never to judge an individual by outward appearance.

It was so strange. Mary had just been issued with a few directives; no query, 'would you like?' or 'does that suit you?'. The directives left no room for argument and Mary murmured, 'All right, Alison?'. Alison nodded and departed with the new friend. It only occurred to Mary later, when Alison was out of sight, that it was a peculiar and outrageous thing to do—to hand her beloved Alison over to a complete stranger. Utterly dejected, she returned to the hospital.

For twelve, long nights, she slept on a truckle bed in a linen room. She was given a cup of tea in the morning and ate snacks from outside. The infirmary was supported by charity and, even had they so wished, they could not afford to feed relatives.

Each evening, at five o'clock, she telephoned the village policeman, as arranged. It had been unsatisfactory for Alison, or the Gordons, to go to the police station. Sometimes, the message had not come through, or the officer was out. After receiving the message, he would cycle up to the house—to report, mostly, 'no change'; but after nine long, harrowing days, 'conscious at times', and, on the twelfth evening, 'fully conscious' and that Alison's mother would return on the following afternoon.

'I'll take you back in the trap about five o'clock, because your mother will need your company. We have all loved having you, Alison, and when things are better, we shall be in touch again.'

What could they do but thank her?

'Some day, we shall help them, Alison. How strange that Mrs. Gordon should have been there, just when we were so confused.'

They fell into each other's arms. 'Daddy is still very ill, Alison, but there is hope, now, and we must just keep on praying for his recovery. I have been allowed to come back to you on condition that I go in each day. We can leave together as you go to school and you must just wait for me in the evening.'

Indeed, Alison had prayed every day, and most of the day, for twelve long days, for the recovery of her beloved father and she was quite convinced, when he was able to return home, that it was the direct answer to prayer, because a very strange thing had happened to Davie.

It had been fortunate for Davie, in one way, that he kept relapsing into unconciousness, for he was taken down several times to the theatre, his wound cleaned and tubes replaced so that the flesh would not grow over them. No chloroform was given, it led to too much sickness. The pain was so intense that he was glad to fade into oblivion.

During a period of semi-consciousness, he was convinced that he lay on the ridge of a pointed wall. This was so painful, he wished to roll off. When his head turned to the right, there were great stretches of lush meadows and a vast carpet of the most beautiful flowers. He could hear his own lark singing, and clearly saw the beech trees beckoning. Then, something made him look to the left and there was an endless waste of ashes, and in the middle stood Mary and Alison, hand in hand. He wanted so much to fall into the flowers, to be nearer the lark, but he knew that he could not abandon those most dear to him. To his very real regret, he turned to the ashes—to the world.

Later, when she heard it, Alison knew what to make of that story. She kept silence, knowing that her fervent prayers had called him back. When she was older she wondered, with the full knowledge of what he had suffered, whether it would not have been kinder to let him go.

Davie was the wonder of the infirmary. At that time, the medics had never seen such a serious case of peritonitis, recover. When he was stronger, Davie had an endless procession of doctors, students, visiting surgeons, who came to 'have a look'. Later, he used to joke with Mary: 'It's the only record I'll ever make—being "written up" in the medical journal.'

He became Sister Stern's pet patient. Because his recovery was so long and so slow, Mary was allowed to bring in port wine and this was locked away by Sister. Every morning at eleven o'clock, after the doctors' round, Davie was handed a medicine glass with the wine. The measure never varied, it was always two tablespoonsful, and the staff nurse would say: 'Come on now, Mr. Cameron, take your medicine and don't be difficult.' The odd thing was that, after leaving hospital and all his life long, Davie could never touch port wine, the very smell of it gave him nausea.

For Alison, life had been especially difficult. When Mary had been permitted to return home, it was on condition that she returned each day, and the authorities had no idea of the difficulties this imposed.

February was one of the wettest months on record, and a three mile walk to the station and back each day in the soaking rain, was in itself an ordeal. Mr. Reith was very kind and took her sometimes on a Saturday, but he was doing Davie's job and had his own family commitments. Mary was more than grateful that she was being paid each week. Naturally, she became ill. Her constitution had never been robust and the recent strain proved too much.

Alison asked one of the mill girls, who passed along the lane, to give the doctor a measage. He came the following morning.

'Pleurisy.'

The doctor, very kind, could not realise the position. He had a maid, a housekeeper, a chauffeur. He patted Alison on the head saying: 'A fire in the bedroom and keep her on light diet.' He added, 'Now, go up to the licensed grocer's near the bridge and fetch half a bottle of brandy.' Taking her mother's purse, off she trotted. The cloak of responsibility had indeed fallen upon her, but if Daddy could hammer in a blacksmith's shop at eleven, she could look after her parents. She certainly knew what a light diet was.

Although they had now lived in the district for some weeks, she knew nobody apart from Mr. Reith and the doctor. She entered the tiny shop.

'May I have a half-bottle of brandy, please?'

A tall, forbidding figure in black, with screwed-back hair and steel-rimmed glasses on the end of her nose, said, outraged:

'Brandy? Indeed, you may not. I never heard of such a thing.'

'I have the money here.'

'It's not the question of money. How old are you?'

'Eleven.'

'And who sent you for brandy, I'd like to know?'

'The doctor.'

'Which doctor?'

'Dr. Grant.'

'Why?'

'My mother is very ill and my father is in hospital.'

'Where do you live?'

'Near the mill.'

Alison could no longer keep the tremor from her voice. She was cold, hungry and dejected. She had not expected an inquisition.

At this point, another, almost identical, figure appeared from the back shop.

'Lottie, you had best put on your hat and cape, and go to find out. It must be that new family at the mill.'

So, carrying the half-bottle of brandy, Lottie set out with Alison to walk the mile-and-a-half back to the Mill House.

It was all true. As so often with Northerners, her stern exterior belied a loving heart.

What sister Annie of the back shop was thinking, Alison wondered several times, because Lottie remained for two-and-a-half hours.

She lit the range, carried coals and sticks up to the bedroom, made a light meal for Mary and Alison, looked in the larder, then took her departure just before darkness fell.

'Keep your mother warm, Alison. I'll be down in the morning.'

Lottie came each day, bringing meat and groceries, until Mary was over the worst; then Alison managed to cope. The most difficult bit of all was to keep the seriousness of Mary's illness from Davie, who was still in a very weak condition. She could not visit him every day, but she went three times a week to the hospital. She explained to Sister why her mother could not come.

'On no account, must you tell your father the truth, Alison. Just say that your mother has a heavy cold, later we will tell him influenza.'

Another problem was food for Davie. She could manage clean pyjamas and towels for him, but a few 'delicacies', as Sister suggested, was more difficult. Lottie still came several times a week, bringing meat and groceries, and she said: 'Don't worry, we'll manage something.'

The hospital, being supported by voluntary contributions, could only supply the most basic food—and that was not really palatable. Now that he was eating a little, Lottie would cook chicken or ham, or tongue, and, between plates, Alison would take a few slices, together with thin bread and butter, and often a little bowl of stewed apples or his favourite sago. What Davie did not eat, others were glad to have.

In all, Alison had been off school for nearly ten weeks, so that posed another problem.

When Davie became suspicious, after the absence of Mary for several weeks, Sister always came to the rescue.

'Your wife has got over this serious bout of "influenza", Mr. Cameron, but we certainly don't want her in here, as long as there is a danger of infection.'

As he grew stronger, he wrote little notes. 'How are you, darling? I will be home soon, there is still a lot of life in this old horse yet.'

Meggie, of course, had visited Davie on several occasions, but it was a difficult cross-country journey for her. When she did come, she brought a large box of eggs, butter, oatcakes and cream for the ward. Sister was more than grateful.

'I really must learn to drive the car,' she thought, 'it would save me so much time.'

Ross, too, paid many visits. To begin with, just to stand and look sorrowfully at his unconscious friend, but later, when he learnt that Mary was ill, he visited on the days Alison could not. When Mary finally managed to visit Davie, he was sitting in a chair, looking the mere shadow of himself but smiling. After almost four months, he was allowed to go home.

'We shall both get stronger, if we are at home together, Mary.'

So, one lovely day in early summer, Mr. Reith brought Davie home in his Humber. Mary accompanied him, carrying a warm blanket. He had a touching send-off from the hospital staff.

'Come and see us in one year, Mr. Cameron. None of us believed that you could survive such extensive peritonitis. You are a living miracle.'

'I know it,' said Davie.

Mary had invited Sister Stern to come and visit them one day, she admired and respected her for all her difficult and often thankless work.

So, on the day of his arrival, Lottie and Alison had the bed ready and Davie's favourite food in the oven.

'I never thought I'd see this day, Mary. I'm glad I did not know you were so ill.'

'How can we ever repay you, Mr. Reith?'

'When you are strong enough, I'll pile the work on!'

'Lottie, we cannot thank you enough.'

'Just let Alison visit us often, in the shop.'

And later, at bedtime:

'Alison, I am very proud of you.'

He went back to work too soon, of course, and had to be half-carried home again, but even the smell of caustic soda had given him pleasure.

So, life began again with great happiness. In time, Sister Stern did visit them, but not as they had expected. Life did indeed hold surprises. When the lonely Ross had visited the unconscious Davie, he had surprised a look of great compassion on the Sister's face, as she felt for his pulse. She just shook her head and looked so disappointed and so vulnerable. He had heard from Mary, how poor the food was in hospital and it occurred to him that the staff, also, must be inadequately fed. So, he started to bring choice cuts of meat, and said, in apparent innocence:

'I hear that you have your own flat, Sister. I have a great favour to ask of you.'

'I'm too busy to favour anyone, Mr. Ross.'

'Well, Sister, I just happen to have some choice steak here. If you would accept it and cook it, perhaps my friend Davie could have a morsel now and then.'

He could hear the starch crackle, but he could tell she didn't really mind; the nerve of it!

Then, one day: 'You need fresh air, Sister, cooped up all day in hospital. Would you permit me to take you for an outing?'

Out of uniform she was a completely different person. Not strict and forbidding, which was the face she showed the world, but kind and thoughtful, and she was called Rosemary.

After Davie left, Ross called again.

'I'm so grateful for all you did for my friend. He is getting on so well, now.'

'His recovery was little short of a miracle.'

'Would you care to see him now, I'm sure that he and Mary would be delighted?'

So, one day a few weeks later, although Ross had said he would visit them, it was a complete surprise to find Rosemary with him at the door.

'You invited each of us, Mary, so we thought we should come together.'

'What a marvellous surprise!'

A few months later, they married. Alison was bridesmaid. Mary and Davie were so happy for them both.

'I'm glad something good came out of my experience in that hospital! Mary, Mr. Reith has been so kind to us—when I think of all the money he has paid you, yet I worked only two weeks for him.'

'He told me that he knew you were the most experienced paper-maker in the trade and he was determined to keep you.'

'It is so pleasant here in Bervie. I hope we stay here for life. Now, I have got the measure of the machines and their best speeds for different types of paper. Surely, we can put roots down here.'

Later that summer, Alan and Linda visited them in their northern outpost. Alan walked very well, as long as it was not too far. He was very disappointed that he could not drive a car, but he had heard that, soon, a special new handbrake was to be fitted for ex-soldiers like himself. He and Linda were very happy with their small business. It was so good to live in a cool climate and not to toil in a factory. He could recommend the life to Davie.

'I must say, in the past, I, too, have been tempted to quit the trade, Alan, but, at last, I have found Bervie. As you know, I have met with great kindness here, so I feel settled.'

6

The last day he had to report to hospital—nearly two years after his illness—they passed the Lea showroom, where they had bought their motor-cycle with Ross. Right in the centre of the window stood their dream car.

'Didn't we have fun with that motorbike, Mary?'

'Fun, yes, after you twice landed us in the ditch—but I loved it. It was as well we sold it when we did—Alison is now too big to squeeze into the sidecar.

'Look, Mary, a two or three-seater Stellite and with a dickey-seat for two.'

'Yes, a lovely shade of blue-grey isn't it?'

'Don't look at the colour, look at the machine!'

'Don't look at all, Davie, it is too tempting.'

The salesman came to the entrance.

'Do come and look, there is no obligation to buy.'

It really was a little beauty, with brass radiator, lights and horn—a spare wheel strapped to the side and a box to hold a spare two-gallon tin of petrol.

'Out of the question for us, dear—three hundred pounds—that is a terrible price. We could get a Ford for one hundred and twenty-five pounds.'

'True, but there is no comparison is there, Davie? Anyway, you couldn't crank it, that would kill you.'

They were both hooked from the moment they entered the shop, and the salesman knew it.

'Why is this car so much more expensive?' asked Davie. 'Just double the price of several others.'

'Well, the others are mass-produced, this one is hand-finished. Look at the engine. It has, also, a self-starter and dynamo lighting.'

'Self-starter?'

'Indeed. A cranking handle is provided but should never be necessary.'

As they had done years ago with Ross, they 'went for a walk'.

'Less would do us, Mary. Three hundred pounds would mean every penny of our savings, even the remains of our nest egg from Rawnpore.'

'Yes, but after all we have suffered, it would be a wonderful "fillip". Let's be devils, Davie, "nothing venture, nothing win".'

'Who is the spendthrift now, I'd like to know?'

So, they bought their first car. No-one could ever accuse them of being stick-in-the-mud.

When they arrived home, Davie was weak at the knees and had to have his milk laced with brandy.

'That nest egg was supposed to be for Alison's education, Mary.'

'Don't worry, I'll make it up. I have a good idea.'

'What?'

'Well, if you don't mind, I will ask Mr. Reith to lease me a part of the field next to the house. I have always been interested in poultry, as you noticed at Linaird. With a little outlay, to have proper hen-houses, up off the ground, with a little ladder for the chickens to climb up . . .'

'Ladder for the chickens. Is my hearing correct?'

'I would also like electric light installed.'

'Electric light in a hen-house? Mary, you're joking!'

'I am not. I have been buying "Poultry World" for a while, with this in mind, before your illness. Breeders have been saying that you can have fresh eggs all the year round if you give the birds a hot mash, after dark, in winter. Then, we would not have to bother with these great crocks of waterglass to preserve eggs for the winter.'

Davie was astounded. The whole affair was well thought out. Mary was still enthusing.

'I would pay myself for all our household eggs and sell the remainder.'

As has already been demonstrated, Mr. Reith was an exceptional man.

'God bless my soul! Electric light for the hens' dinner-time, what next?'

He was highly amused. You can have a large section of the field next to your garden and the rent will be one dozen fresh eggs at Christmas.

The whole undertaking was such a success that two local farmers came to have a look and actually bought fresh eggs from Mary in January—unheard of in the frost and snow of that area, at that period of time. By the following year, they had their own electric light installed. When Meggie and Peter came to visit, they were much impressed.

'You see, Davie, I will replace the Stellite tyres as I promised!'

That little Stellite brought them, and many of their friends, endless joy. It never stuck on hills, it never caused any trouble. Davie kept the engine as clean as on the day of its production and Alison polished the brass to earn pocket money. That was no mean feat. All the Stellite required was petrol, oil, water and tyres.

There was only one difficulty with the poultry. A big black Leghorn cock, very conscious of his shimmering green tail feathers, with an enormous comb and huge spurs, somehow or other got through the wire mesh, through the hedge and took up an aggressive stance in the middle of one of the lanes, leading to the mill. The girls from the finishing house always took the lane because it saved them ten precious minutes, morning and evening. On several mornings they were late and, on enquiry, Davie found that they could not get past the cock. It ran at them and pecked at their legs, even jumped at them. They were terrified. Something drastic had to be done. Mary had clipped one of his wings so that he could not fly at the girls, but he still got out. In the end, he had to be killed. He was a huge bird and had never threatened Alison, nor any of their friends. They just could not put him in their own pot, so a label was simply tied round his leg and he was delivered twenty-four hours later to Jane and George, who now lived in a new semi-detached house on a hill above Port-Glasgow.

The Stellite was wonderful, life was wonderful, and so was Bervie

They visited Meggie and Peter one Sunday in the month, Ross and Rosemary another, and they spent holidays based in Port-Glasgow or with Alan and Linda in Oakley.

Yes, the chickens were a great success. Mary kept several varieties—in separate houses. She had Wyandottes and Buff Orpingtons for table birds and black or white Leghorns for laying. When she had broodie hens, she exchanged settings of eggs with Meggie, or with local farmers, she sent for day-old chickens, the whole thing became an obsession. She could have run a poultry farm, of free range hens, single-handed.

'You do give yourself a lot of trouble, Mary. You only wanted a few chickens, when you started, now you are even talking of turkeys—it is too much.'

'It is my hobby, Davie, and I do save money from it.'

'Yes, but it is beginning to interfere with the little free time we have. I don't think you should buy this incubator you speak of.'

It was only over the poultry that Alison ever heard Davie sound cross and she thought he was justified.

One Saturday, they had planned to meet Ross and Rosemary to have a picnic at the seaside.

Instead of just scattering grain this summer afternoon and giving them fresh water, Mary had to make a mash with poultry spice and all the extras. She could have prepared it in the morning. Suddenly, hens were becoming more important than people. Mary had kept them late on several Saturdays. Davie and Alison would be ready, waiting, having done the clearing away and washing up—Mary would put her hat on as though she, too, were ready—but no, she must start on a mash. Davie had joked about it for several Saturdays but today he was annoyed. They would be so late for the picnic.

'Mary, we must go now. Ross and Rosemary will be waiting. Give the hens grain!'

'I can't keep chickens and not look after them.'

'Well, it's the chickens or us today, Mary.'

'Then go—both of you. I don't mind!'

To her utter amazement, Davie and Alison got into the car and did go. But Davie stopped the car a mile from the house, and sat for an hour, then returned. Alison said nothing. She felt miserable. All her sympathy was with her father, but she could see how unhappy he was. He loved her mother so.

On their return, they found Mary sitting on the seat, in tears, her hat all askew. She flew into his arms and all he said was:

143

'I couldn't go without you, Mary.'

'I was stupid. I'll come now.'

Ross and Rosemary had given them up, they were so late. They were anxious, also, for Davie was always such a punctual person.

'I'm so sorry, Ross and Rosemary. I just could not get away any earlier today.'

The poultry decreased rapidly in numbers. Nobody remarked on it.

It was incongruous, too, that there was electric light in the hen-house but no such things as plugs for radiators nor an electric iron, nor hot water in the bath. Yet, the cold, dry winters suited them all.

When Alan and Linda came on holiday, the following year, they brought a wonderful gift with them—a wireless—a large, bobbin-shaped piece of wood with a coil of wire round the middle and a crystal fixed on top. On a lever, beside it, was fixed a very fine wire which he called a 'cat's whisker'. He explained that you had to move this whisker very gently to different parts of the crystal, to tune in. Then, metal earphones were put on to enable the listener to hear the music or the talk being broadcast through the ether. It was miraculous—yet they had no telephone.

They were all so happy. Davie was making the finest white writing paper, watermarked 'Aurora', along with parchments, vellums, coated magazine papers. They only had to open their windows to hear the lark sing or the curlews cry. There was trout fishing two hundred yards from the house and Alison rode to school on a light, three-geared bicycle.

The shock was all the greater, therefore, when Mr. Reith's house-keeper knocked on their door very early one morning, to say that he had had a heart attack and died in the night.

They were shattered. They had loved him. He had been bright and cheerful, as usual, when Davie saw him the day before and he was only fifty years of age.

All the employees mourned him most sincerely and waited to see what would happen. The mill carried on as usual, there were many orders to supply.

The mill was entailed. Mr. Reith's heir was a cousin who knew little about the paper trade, in a practical sense. He was a pulp importer and he engaged a team of associates, an industrial chemist, an ex-Colonel of the Guards, an actuary and two gentlemen of means. They formed the board and after their first meeting, Davie was called in. The Colonel had been appointed managing director, and said with condescension:

'You have carried on very well, Cameron, and we are grateful. We have made Mr. Graham, our industrial chemist, works overseer, so you will be answerable to him in future.'

'Mary, it's dreadful. I never would have believed that the death of one man could have changed the whole atmosphere and structure of the mill. They only want to make a million, they have no interest in the quality of our "Aurora". Several key men are leaving and I feel I must do the same.'

'It is sad, Davie, we were all so happy here.'

'Mr. Reith was a friend in need and this was an oasis when we needed it most.'

Davie was well known in the trade now, and all he had to do was to inform two talkative travellers that he was seeking a change of mill.

Alison, now eighteen, had done well in her examinations and had applied for acceptance to the University at Duncross. So, if they had to move, now was the time.

7

By the end of the summer, Davie was offered a managerial post in a small town in central Scotland, almost equidistant between Edinburgh and Glasgow. It was a small industrial town, not in any way attractive—poles apart from Bervie. Indeed, to the Camerons, it seemed a cement jungle and the house they were offered temporarily, was a big Victorian building which had, at one time, had a beautiful garden. However, for years, the mill had been encroaching on the land, now there remained only a large area of tufted grass at one side and, on the other, wide entrance gates and a drive bordered by lawns and bushes, but all the front windows looked at the huge brick wall of the finishing house. There was a side door from the grass into the machine house. It was a handsome house in the wrong place and it was most depressing from both outside and inside.

'We have been promised one of the new houses on the hill, Mary, so try not to be too downhearted.'

'Yes, Davie, but we don't have it in writing.'

'At least we are still together. It is splendid that Alison has got a transfer to Glasgow University. The train service is very good.'

It had taken much soul-searching to accept the post, but the salary was substantial and all the extras of coal, house and electricity were important. They needed the money to put Alison through University. Davie would have to pay for every pencil and sheet of paper.

'She is to have all the education she is fit for, Mary.'

They needed a car, too, to get away from the smoke and grime and concrete. The Stellite had been sold and they now had a four-seater Clyno.

The house had, at least, many labour saving gadgets which Mary had never had before. As well as the big old range, there was a gas cooker, electrical points all through the house for vacuum cleaner, lamps, radiators and, joy of joys, an excellent hot water system. These were the small compensations.

They were nearer to Jane, George and the rest of the family, but farther from Meggie and Peter, Ross and Rosemary.

'We shall only stay until Alison has qualified, then we shall look for another Bervie.'

It was a large mill with two machines constantly turning out newsprint.

'It is easier to produce newsprint than finer papers, Davie?'

'Newsprint has its pitfalls also. As a matter of fact, there is a complaint to be investigated this afternoon. We are being criticised because the print is blurred on the newspaper.'

'Is it the paper?'

'Definitely not, but we must prove this.'

'Can you?'

'Yes, I think our own chemist has the answer. It lies in the quality of the ink.'

When visitors came, the men would congregate in one room and, in exasperation, Mary would say: 'If you have made enough tons of paper for today, do come and eat!'

The men of the trade formed a sort of fraternity, each one knew a man in other mills up and down the country. Competition, throughout Britain, was very keen. Prices were cut, wages were still low. In a management position in such a big concern, Davie could easily have made money, but he was as honest as the daylight.

'Buy our product and there is a percentage for the one who gives the order.'

'Oh yes, I'll let you know.'

But the order always went to the firm selling the best article at the best price, be it felts, wires, paint, woodpulp or esparto.

If a case of whisky or port was delivered at Christmas, Davie handed out one bottle to each foreman, or machineman, keeping one for himself. It was the same with cigars or cigarettes—he didn't smoke, so the workers received them. He was well aware that some travellers said: 'He is a damn fool, he'll never have a bean, he is too honest.' But Davie did 'get on', if slowly and laboriously. No quick rise to lucrative heights. Just a steady plodding and merit that had to be acknowledged. Some called him 'a soft touch'. Indeed, he was always so. A man, off sick, had only to say 'I can't pay the rent and the wife is sick.'

In the evening, Mary would say: 'No, Davie, we can't afford it, give him ten shillings.'

It was a good thing that Davie never carried money except on Saturdays, when they went to town.

'Just as well I control the cash, Alison, your father would have us in the poorhouse.'

Alison had early learnt to say, 'I don't like it'—especially on holiday. Once, in St. Anne's, when she was eighteen—now attractive, in a neat, tailored way, never pretty but definitely with a touch of 'class'—they were window shopping. Alison had lingered at one boutique where there was a beautiful leopard skin jacket in the window:

'You would look nice in that, Alison,' said Davie. 'Let's ask the price.'

'No, Dad, I don't like it. I couldn't wear it where we live, it would be smutty in no time.'

Deflated, Davie looked at Mary, but Mary had trained Alison well.

'It's a good thing she doesn't like it, her fees have to be paid when we go back.'

One couldn't call Davie spendthrift, he was just overgenerous to other people. All his life, his womenfolk had to protect him from this trait. As well as overgenerous, Davie was overtrusting—as, indeed, was Mary.

They lived in an unsalubrious area, the new house 'up the hill' never having materialised.

One cold January day, at the local shopping area, Mary saw a slip of a girl gazing at the twopenny hot pies in a baker's shop, with the longing of real hunger.

'Are you hungry?'

'Not half.'

'Here you are then, go and get yourself two hot pies.'

Although she was not usually impulsive, she said: 'I need help in the house . . . I wonder . . . have you got a job?'

The girl shook her head, she had not taken time to say 'thank you' but her large dark eyes were full of gratitude.

'How old are you?'

'Sixteen.'

'Would you be interested in helping me?'

A vigorous nod was the answer, as she went on chewing.

'You had better go home and ask your parents and if they agree, then come tomorrow morning about nine o'clock. I'll give you seventeen shillings weekly and you will have a nice big room to yourself.'

Off the kitchen, on the ground floor, was a large bedroom, obviously meant for two or three beds, with a handsome mahogany wardrobe, a large dressing table and a chest of drawers. The two wide windows were barred because the room was on the ground floor. A passage, at a right angle from the kitchen, let to a bathroom, laundry, storeroom and coalhouse. Halfway along the passage was a massive Victorian door with an enormous lock and key.

'Well, Agnes, we'll go into town now, to fit you out.'

'Fit me out? What with?'

'Working clothes, an afternoon dress, a coat and underclothing—not to mention a toothbrush.'

Never had a family received greater kindness from a maid. Agnes was a worker. The kitchen was spotless, she was neat and tidy. Nothing was too much trouble. She had to be forced to take her afternoon off.

'Maybe she has nowhere to go,' said Davie.

'She said, she lived with a brother and his wife.'

'Perhaps she is not welcome there.'

'Agnes, why don't you take the afternoon and evening off?'

'I don't like my brother, he always wants my money.'

'Well, take only a little money with you, leave the rest here.'

Agnes' big black eyes surveyed her with commiseration. They surely said: 'You don't know what you are talking about.'

Indeed, this would have been the reading, had Alison foreseen the future.

Towards the end of the Christmas term, she was studying intensively and always worked better after the household had gone to bed. About half-past-one in the morning, she crept downstairs in the dark to raid the larder, she was so hungry. How strange! She had heard her father switch off the lights in the passage. Agnes had gone to bed at eight o'clock.

'Curious that a girl of sixteen would want to go to bed so early each night,' remarked Davie one evening.

'Agnes, bring your sewing or knitting and sit with us and listen to the radio.'

'No thank you, Mrs. Cameron. I like to go to bed early, I read.'

Remembering all this, Alison reached the foot of the staircase and switched on the hall light—almost simultaneously, the light in the kitchen corridor went out. Alison literally felt the hair rising at the back of her neck. Someone was there.

'Is that you, Agnes?'

No reply. It would be folly to go farther, so Alison beat a hasty retreat upstairs to reluctantly awaken her father. After a whispered conversation, the comical procession began. Davie, clutching a long, brass poker, led the way, closely followed by Mary with tongs, and Alison with her tennis racquet. Solemnly and furtively, they crept downstairs, through the hall, down the three steps to the kitchen corridor, then Davie switched the light on. There was nobody to be seen. A quick visit to Agnes' bedroom—there she lay, seemingly sound asleep, but Davie found the heavy back door unlocked—the key on the outside. He knew that he had locked up at ten o'clock.

Not to worry Mary, whose nerves had been shattered by her experiences in Rawnpore, Davie said: 'I must have been careless and forgotten to lock up and you, Alison, must have imagined the light. Why were you up so late, anyway?'

'Strange that Sandy did not bark,' said Mary.

Next morning, two weeks before Christmas, all was made plain. At seven o'clock there was no fire in the range, no kettle on the boil—such a miserable, cold, wet December morning. On opening Agnes' door, Mary found a note on the pillow—'Sorry, Mrs. Cameron, you were all O.K. We left you one turkey for Christmas.'

That was the final blow. As well as chickens, Mary had reared seven turkeys in a corner of the garden—turkeys, mostly, as gifts for relatives and friends. At daylight, all three proceeded to the poultry houses—not a chicken, not an egg, only one lonely turkey peering through the wire mesh.

The police had to be told and, on enquiry, they found that Agnes was related to a Glasgow gang called the 'Forty Thieves'. Agnes and the leader had disappeared.

The police officer asked, 'And why do you have coal piled over the dyke in the potato field? The farmer has been complaining?'

Agnes had been slight of figure, but she had thrown a vast amount of coal over the wall. A large cache of jars of jam, pickles, preserves of all kinds, were found behind the huge wardrobe.

'Alison must have disturbed them, when they left all that food behind.'

'No wonder she always went to bed so early, she was busy.'

Much was explained when later, one evening before Christmas, Alison answered a knock on the back door. There stood a young man, quite a 'smasher' and wearing the string muffler of his type, with a 'hooker doon'—a cap pulled well over the eyes.

'Where's Aggie?'

'Gone.'

'Rubbish! Gone! We are to be married on Saturday.'

Davie, as usual, was softhearted:

'You said she was kind to you, Mary.'

'Yes, and she worked very hard. Besides, she touched nothing of our personal possessions—not jewellery, not money. All that, is intact.'

'So, it was food and coal, and all the poultry.'

'She did leave us our Christmas dinner,' said Alison.

'It is obvious that the gang leader forced her to take what she did. Alison must have disturbed them coming in for the jams and preserves.'

They had never liked the house—a barrack of a place. Mary's nerves got worse. She could not be in the house alone, after dark, especially after Alison's second experience.

Davie, also, was too trusting. When he took this post, it had been clearly understood that they would be expected to live in that house, only until a suitable one could be found on the hill, away from the factories. But, as usual, it was a gentleman's agreement, a promise, a handshake—no move was made to find a new house.

'It is too handy for the works, here, Davie. You are on call night and day. The directors know that you have only to slip through that little door.'

The following February, one misty lunch-time Davie said: 'Happy birthday, Mary, I have tickets for Matheson Lang in "The Chinese Bungalow". Alison says she can't come, she has too much work to do, so they are for the matinée. We can have a meal afterwards.'

Since they were within a short train ride of many good theatres in Edinburgh and in Glasgow, Mary and Davie had become keen devotees. Every time a really interesting play was produced, they were there.

It had been quite an effort to get Davie to enter a cinema. He had remembered the days of the magic lantern, the flickering shots of the early movies, so he just refused to go. It was by subterfuge that Alison got him there. It had been her twenty-first birthday and she wanted to see 'Sorrell & Son'. When asked what she would like to do, she said 'apart from a small party at home' she would like to 'do a show and have supper out'.

'All right, you will be in town, get the tickets, Alison.'

When the night arrived and Davie found himself at the entrance to the cinema, he was hurt, very hurt. He felt cheated, but Mary's gentle voice whispered, 'Don't spoil her treat, Davie, put up with it for once.'

That was Davie hooked to talkies, musical comedies, musical hall, drama—the lot. It was all so different from the quiet, country pursuits he had always known.

So, when the day for this particular matinée arrived, Alison was alone in the big house.

After the Aggie episode, there was no more heart ruling head. A very reliable daily was their friend and helper. She had left about three o'clock. Davie and Mary were already at the matinée. It was a grey February day, when early morning mist had given way to slight fog. Alison was struggling with a difficult essay on Moral Philosophy, when the doorbell rang. She had the little dressing-room over the hall, as a study, so looked out. In the slight mist, she saw a figure standing behind a laurel bush, near the door. When, therefore, she went down to answer the bell, she had the sense to put the chain on the door. A well dressed young man said, politely: 'Good afternoon, I have come to repair you sewing-machine. I'm from "Singers".'

'There is nothing wrong with our machine.'

'Just a moment,'—fingering through a few sheets of paper. 'Oh, sorry, not repair. It says here, to electrify your old model.'

'Strange, we already have an all electric model.'

Alison managed to close the door just as a foot was moving to keep it open. She turned the key in the lock and went upstairs. One man at the door, another behind the laurel—she went into the bathroom and looked into the field—of coal notoriety—and saw a third man sitting on the wall. Clearly they had expected the house to be empty. The telephone was downstairs. One had to ring through the mill switchboard until five o'clock, then the telephone was plugged directly to the post office switchboard. No reply—definitely no reply. For the first time, Alison felt trapped. The office had forgotten to switch over.

It was getting dark, she could no longer see the two men near the door. She went to the bathroom window again. She was beginning to shake. Suddenly, the man jumped off the wall and ran down a back lane. Just then the doorbell rang, and to Alison's intense relief she heard her father shouting: 'Alison, come and take this chain off.'

Mary had had a headache and did not feel like eating out. Davie had to go to the mill office, to plug in the telephone, before he could call the police.

When contacted, 'Singers' said that they would never send three men to look at one machine and would certainly give notice of a man coming to do a job on one of their machines.

'Davie, I can't stay in this house much longer, it is getting me down.'

'I know, Mary. Tomorrow, I'll give an ultimatum—either the firm keeps its promise about a more suitable house, or I go.'

He thought, 'Just as well that Alison did not tell her mother that, only the previous week, she had met a strange woman coming DOWN their staircase, saying sweetly: 'I just wanted to use your toilet'. But the same woman took to her heels, ran down the avenue and jumped into a waiting car.

With hindsight, in later years, Davie remembered that nobody in that town had done them any physical injury, had not even threatened to do so—then, cynically for him, 'Of course, there was the threat of corporal punishment then.'

Davie was truly disillusioned about the house question. The managing director had said: 'We think very highly of you, Cameron, and would like to buy you a new house, but we are in a recession, it is 1930, and there is mass unemployment.'

Then there was the question of young trainees. There were four of them—all public school boys related to, or friends of, some of the directors.

In a few years, would they supplant him—having training but no experience? This was the psychological moment when fate, or the financier, intervened.

8

He was a well-known figure in the City of London and had interests all over the country.

'I have just been in Glasgow on business and thought I might call on you, Cameron. You will remember we met at the last newsprint conference?'

'Oh, yes,' said Davie, privately wondering: 'Why should he call at my house in the evening, instead of at my office in daytime?'

After Mary had provided refreshments, he said, 'I'll get to the point Mr. Cameron. It is well known, in papermaking circles, that you are the best practical man in the trade. You have experience of all grades of papers.'

'Flattery?' wondered Davie, but said nothing, just looked hard with his bright, expressive eyes.

'Do you wish to talk business?'

'Yes, but I would like Mrs. Cameron and your daughter to remain.'

'Subtle,' decided Davie.

'With a few friends, I have bought a large mill in the south of England, which is sliding rapidly towards failure and bankruptcy. You are in your prime, at the peak of your experience. If you were willing to enter into a contract with us, to manage the mill, it would be well worth your while. In these years of unemployment, you would save the jobs of fifteen hundred men and women. You would have complete authority over the mill and the manpower. You would have eight hundred pounds per annum to begin with, with free house, coal and light, but the important part is, if you can make the mill pay, you will receive one half of one per cent of the profits. That, in the future, could make you a very rich man.

'Hmm. I must discuss this with my wife.'

Looking at all three, the financier said, 'I trust you will all keep this proposition in the strictest confidence. When you make a decision, telephone this number and I shall send you a written offer of the post.' Turning to Alison, 'My dear young lady, think of the opportunities for you, if your father came south.'

'Aye,' thought Davie, 'worming his way into the apple of my eye.'

'I rely on you to persuade your father.'

That was a Friday, so the whole week-end was spent in discussion. Every pro and con was considered.

'Unemployment is rife, it is a good offer, and we are ready to go.'

'I can't stand this house any longer. I'd like to go to the south of England. It was lovely in Maidenhead, all those years ago.'

'What about Alison?'

'Don't think of me. I shall be abroad this coming year. When I return to do my finals in two years, I can take a room, or perhaps get into a hostel. I shall be home for the long vacations.'

'This half of one per cent,' said Mary, 'he won't put that in writing?'

'No, I shouldn't think so, that is dependent on the mill making a profit.'

'Still, Davie, it should be in writing. You have been caught before.'

'With a salary like that, we could save money for our old age. I won't get a state pension, having been classed as a "white collar" worker.'

Alison had the final rational question:

'Why don't you both go down and see the place?'

'True,' said Davie, 'there is no point in moving, if the machines are tied up with string.'

The acceptance was a foregone conclusion.

The present board of directors were aghast.

'We will give you eight hundred pounds and a new house immediately. You can't leave us, Cameron.'

'Your offer of a house is about four years too late, gentlemen. I have accepted.'

'Strange, isn't it, Mary, how they can always come up with the goods when I decide to depart?'

The new mill was in a poor condition but had great possibilities. The village of Hathstowe was very attractive, with its old houses set in beautiful gardens. Some of the older houses were still thatched. Near the river, on a slight rise, stood the manager's house. It was detached and built of deep red brick. It had four bay windows and June roses climbing round the porch and windows. On this lovely summer day, it captured Mary's heart. The mill was just out of sight, round a bend on the river.

'Oh, Davie, isn't it beautiful? Compare it with the grim old house we are in, at the moment.'

'The only snag is, that we shall be nearly five hundred miles from Alison,' said Davie. 'It is a long, expensive rail journey to visit us.'

'I know, Davie, but she will be abroad for a year, by that time she

154

will be twenty-two—all the woman she will ever be, and she is level-headed.'

'She can come down for all the holidays, that will be nearly five months in the year. I feel we must take the post, Mary.'

'I hope your work will not be too hard, Davie. I certainly love the house and the village.'

The financier, Mr. Newton, was chairman of the new board of directors, and Davie, who was now fifty-three, had a written agreement for seven years, but no written promise of a percentage of profits. Mr. Newton had said that the board, whose members had put most of their own money into the venture, would not agree to this, until they saw profits and what degree of profit.

'We are having a good salary, let's be content with that, meantime.'

New, brisk, energetic engineers were engaged and new key men appointed. By 1933, the three machines were working well, and orders were rolling in.

In 1935, at Davie's suggestion, the board agreed to install another large new machine to make a new paper—glassine. They had had numerous requests from sweet and chocolate factories, as well as from toy manufacturers, for the new paper. To begin with, it was brown and matt; but later, they could supply any colour, plain or glazed. There had been just one snag. It had to be a German machine. Five German engineers came over to install it. They were good, efficient workers, who said that they spoke no English. It took many months to install, and a year before glassine was running on the rollers. Davie thought that one of the young engineers had learnt English very quickly—he had heard him in the local inn chatting to one of their own beaterman. The supervisor, who came to inspect the huge erection, was rather an arrogant individual. However, the machine worked well and did not even have teething troubles.

Glassine? That was new to Davie, but as long as it was paper, Davie would manage. He experimented until he had mastered the art. Always a good colourman, the machine was producing the new paper in every possible colour. He would often walk round the mill in the evening, accompanied by Mary, and would be heard muttering words like, alum, lye, water percentage on the damper, soda ash. The men would nod and smile. It was all in his head. He might jot something down, at a desk, but that was merely an instruction for the relief man coming in.

Mary and Davie were always together. Alison had married soon after she qualified and they were content in each other's affection—a spin for an hour on a hot evening, a picnic by the sea—all holidays spent in the

North with Alison and Iain. They lived just outside Glasgow. Mary and Davie were well pleased with their young son-in-law.

'They love each other as much as we do,' said Mary.

'Think of the good example we have given them,' he would tease.

One Easter, they had an enormous surprise. When Davie received a letter, he went through a routine which used to exasperate Mary and Alison.

'Who is it from?'

No answer. For Davie would touch the tip of the sheet with his tongue, then hold the paper up to the light, then rub it between thumb and forefinger, pronounce judgement as to quality and composition of materials, and, finally, the watermark. Then, he would look at the signature. Only with a letter from Alison, did he read it first.

'Well, I'll be jiggered. It comes from someone called Niz Singh. He says he is the youngest son of Ram and would like to call on us.'

'Of course, he must come. How exciting. Telephone him tonight!'

They met a tall, very pleasant young man at Bristol, and drove him the twenty-five miles back to Hathstowe. He had lots of news about Ram and Asi, who could not write. He, Niz, had always written the postcards. Asi had died two years previously but his sons, together with Ram and his sons, continued to cultivate the land they owned. Indeed, by sharing expenses, they had bought another strip alongside. He, Niz, had won a scholarship to an agricultrual college in England.

'What a wonderful meeting, Niz. How long are you to be in this country?'

'Only five more months, Mrs. Cameron. I had difficulty in finding your address. Also, I would like to visit Mr. Turner.'

'Well, if you have a free week-end, do come again. We shall be very happy to have you.'

'Pay our respects to your parents, Niz, and please keep us informed about them.'

He came once again, and then left for Darjeeling.

'Davie, that life is aeons away.'

'Yes, it would be very different now. Rawnpore has been greatly altered, and has moved with the times.'

The times. That was another worry—1939 was with them, and the horror of World War II. Most of his fine, young men had to go. Older men had to carry on somehow. Young women were engaged to do many of the lighter jobs. Despite the new safety regulations, Davie would not permit them near the machines, nor the cutters, nor the guillotines.

156

The rigours and difficulties of war affected everyone. Davie parted with his beautiful Sunbeam-Talbot.

'It will only deteriorate, even if I have it hung from the garage rafters, and we should not be using petrol for pleasure. If we wish to go to the city, we must go on a day that we can get a lift in a mill lorry.

Indeed, one weekday in the spring of 1942, they did just that. They had been given a lift by one of the works' vehicles as far as Bath. They had not had a day off for months, and had decided to do some shopping. Davie was sitting in the square, admiring the flowers and watching the pigeons, when he saw a young woman sit down on the adjoining seat. She read a magazine for a time, then looked at her watch and departed, leaving the magazine on the seat. Davie had lost sight of her—she might even have slipped into the Abbey. He thought, 'What a pity,' then, 'Oh well, some other girl will be lucky enough to find it.' To his surprise, however, a man sat down, picked up the magazine and left, carrying it under his arm. Something kept teasing Davie's brain— it was the young man, he was not in uniform, he had a very slight limp. No, he did not recognise the face, but there was something familiar about him. That was it—the attitude, slightly supercilious, an arrogant toss of the head.

Gradually, he became aware that he had seen this individual before—then a sudden flashback to 1935. When the new glassine machine was being installed, he had remarked, merely to be pleasant, 'Oh, Karl Ernst, you will have the machine running in a few days.' Instead of an affable or jocular reply, the young engineer had said, with scarcely veiled contempt, 'I am the engineer, not you,' and clicked his heels.

Now, why was that cocky young snout walking about Bath seven years later?

'Mary, I'm sure I saw that cocky Karl Ernst, of the glassine machine, not half an hour ago.

'But you couldn't have, Davie, he is German!'

'He has grown a moustache, but I'm sure it was he.'

'Then you should mention it to the authorities.'

'Perhaps better to seem an old fool, than to let the incident pass.'

He went to the police headquarters, saw an intelligence officer, who thanked him and said, 'It is perhaps a good thing that you did not show recognition. If we find him, he will not connect the arrest with you.'

The authorities had to wait several weeks, before anyone of the description appeared again. When he did, his papers were found to be unsatisfactory and, after long interrogation, he was found to be a spy.

This might explain why, after a raid on the Bristol Docks, a plane had dropped a bomb in a field about a mile from the mill. Had it been meant for the glassine machine?

A man in plain clothes called three months later, to thank Davie for being so observant, merely saying: 'Your, guess is as good as mine, Mr. Cameron, as to the result.'

Alison's husband joined the R.N.V.R. and Alison, herself, went to work in a munitions factory.

Just as life seemed to be so good, the whole world had to be rocked by the insanity of a few.

In 1943, Davie had to make his greatest decision. Mr. Newton, the chairman, who was facile with words, called to see him. He was accompanied by another director.

'Cameron, we have a proposition to make.'

Sack? wondered Davie.

'We are entering on hard times. Two young directors have been called up. I have so many commitments in London, I now find it difficult to travel down so often. Will you become our managing director?'

Davie was struck dumb. After a long silence, he managed to say:

'I must have time to think about it.'

'Of course, two days. To put it bluntly, we need you badly on the board. We need a practical man, who knows paper from A to Z. You would, of course, receive director's fees, which would add considerably to your income.'

After a final sip of Davie's Drambuie, they departed.

☆   ☆   ☆

'You look very pale, Davie, what did they want?'

'They have asked me to become managing director of the firm.'

'Oh, Davie,' she breathed, her eyes shining. 'What an honour!'

'Aye, maybe, but I'll not accept.'

'Not accept?'

'No, a man must know his limitations as well as his potential.'

'Limitations?' she whispered.

'Aye. Remember, Mary, that I left school at nine-and-a-half.'

'Yes, but you are self-educated and well-read, and you know more about all classes of papermaking than anyone else in the country.'

'Now, think, my dear. 'I'm an elderly Scot, slow in speech, so that, even with my knowledge, how could I hold my own in a board room against these fellows from Oxford and Cambridge? They would try to tie me in knots with their flow of words.'

'You're doing not so badly right now!'

'I couldn't make a sophisticated speech, wrap it up in tinsel, then present it. No, I know when to stop. Besides, they are only using me, in the meantime, dangling a carrot of fees before my nose. I'm still awaiting my percentage on profits. Put not your trust in financiers, Mary.'

'Do whatever will make you happiest, Davie. You have struggled all your life—just think, from the grinding poverty of the rag-house to an offer of a managing directorship. I just want you to be happy.'

Davie had been polite but terse.

'Gentlemen, I thank you most sincerely for the honour you have accorded me, but I cannot accept your offer.'

He gave no further explanation, just his brilliant smile, and walked from the boardroom. He smiled to himself, he could almost hear them say 'B..... fool, to forgo such an opportunity'.

This did not suit the financier at all. His octopus-like arms were already encircling other factories and he had to have a practical man at board level. Another director was brought in. He had learnt from bush telegraph that he was second choice and he decided to make things 'hot' for Cameron.

Davie toiled on to the end of the war, until the lads came back again. Then, at sixty-nine, decided to retire.

He was tired, and his dear Mary was not so well. He had called in the doctor, because of her nerves and stomach trouble, and he had been told that her heart was causing trouble, also. They had been discussing, when they would go, and where. Thankfully, Iain had returned safely and been demobbed, so they decided to look for a small cottage near Alison. But it was not to be. When Davie came in from work one evening, he found Mary sitting in the armchair, unconscious. She died soon afterwards. He thought of Sarah and the desolation that must have overwhelmed Jimmy in a similar situation.

He just could not believe that he was alone, that his beloved Mary, whom he had loved so devotedly for most of his life and with whom he had shared everything, had gone.

9

Alison asked him where he would like to live. He had spent many years in Hathstowe, but the old vision of Inveraray kept floating before his eyes.

'Well, Dad, when we got our new car recently, we had a run to Loch Fyne and, near the shore, there is an empty cottage. Iain and I loved it and it occurred to us last night, that you might be interested in it. It is very cheap.

That was it. He got rid of all unnecessary furniture. He kept the antique furniture and a few old pieces they had selected with care. These he put into store until required. Mary was rarely out of his mind and, silently, he would commune with her. 'Now, dear, shall I do this or would you prefer it so?' She was always with him and he felt comforted.

It was an L-shaped crofter's cottage, aptly named 'The Shieling'. It had two fields, a small garden and several outhouses. The front windows looked across Loch Fyne towards Strachur but the others, at the side, looked across the loch to the mountains of Argyll. Davie chose this section and, with the help of a local builder, modernised it to comprise a living room, kitchen, bathroom and bedroom. They kept the old oak beams and the stable-door. The steading provided two good garages and his own Austin looked tiny inside.

'You and Iain can have the main cottage, Alison. You might like to have it for week-ends and holidays.'

So, it was arranged. During the week, a cheery little friend 'did for him' and most week-ends Alison and Iain were there. Sandy, the spaniel, loved it.

'In the winter, you will come up to town with us,' they said.

☆   ☆   ☆

Sitting in his car, high up on the forestry road, Davie could see the loch and the high peaks of Glen Croe. 'The Cobbler' was just out of sight. He smiled as he remembered the tales he had been told, as a tiny boy, about the cobbler, his wife Jean, the row they had had, and he had been taken to see a stream trickling down the mountainside, foaming onto the road. It was their 'sour milk burn'.

All was still, except for the buzzing of the bees in the heather and a red squirrel darting up a spruce sapling. Over to his left, was a whole hill covered with rhododendrons. They reminded him, suddenly, of a hill-station in India. What wonderful times he and Mary had spent together! At first, simply revelling in the escape from the heat of the plains, or sitting on the verandah spellbound by the beauty of the night—the deep blue of the sky, the wonderful silvery moonlight—just sitting, holding each other by the hand. Yes, they had known what love meant, true, faithful, abiding love. The ecstasy of it all! Over the years their love had never lessened. After a few hours' separation, they were always thrilled to meet again, to talk, to sit in companionable silence. This wonderful and lasting bond had been a sublimation, beyond understanding.

They had not agreed on everything, of course, that would have been dull. She had been a real tease at times. In this, Alison was like her— but he must stop dreaming of the past. He must try to be happy in his waiting, for waiting he was, to join her. It should not be too long now.

He had completed the circle. Here he was, back where he had begun. He could see the stone dyke on which he had perched when sent as a 'look-out' for Auntie Mabel and her husband, whom she always called 'Thomas D.' At four years of age, he had been put there to watch for strangers.

'If you see anyone coming up the side-road, Davie, you must cut across the fields and tell us.'

Little innocent, he did not know why. Many years later, he learned of that tiny, illicit still.

'It's been a long time since then,' he thought.

What a fight it had been against poverty, against ill-health, against those huge machines, in order to subject them to his will for the production of perfection. But what wonderful friends he had had, when he most needed them, and what a wonderful girl—his Mary!

'Well, the light is fading, I'd better get my rod and go down to the pool. I could just do with a fine trout.'

'In life there remain
Faith, Hope and Love
and the greatest of these
is Love'